ラフカディオ・ハーンの
英作文教育

Lafcadio Hearn's Student Composition Corrections

アラン・ローゼン／西川 盛雄

弦書房

目　次

序文（小泉 凡）……………………………………………………………………4
英文序文（English Foreword）………………………………………………6
経緯と解説 ……………………………………………………………………7
判読と復元の手続 …………………………………………………………10
判読・復元・日本語訳
　「大谷正信」の英作文添削 ……………………………………………………11
　　［1］　The Hototogisu　ホトトギス　12
　　［2］　The Greatest Japanese　最も偉大な日本人　16
　　［3］　The greatest Japanese Part II　最も偉大な日本人 そのII　18
　　［4］　The fire-fly　蛍　20
　　［5］　The mountain called Dai-sen　大山と呼ばれる山　24
　　［6］　The Botan　牡丹　26
　　［7］　Hina matsuri　雛祭り　30
　　［8］　Composition: [What is the most awful thing?]
　　　　　作文：［世に最も怖いものは何か？］　34
　　［9］　Ghosts　幽霊　44
　　［10］　The Birthday of His Majesty　天皇誕生日　48
　　［11］　Composition: [Creator]　作文：［創造者］　52
　　［12］　Boating on the lake of Shinji　宍道湖をボートで行くこと　56
　　［13］　The Tortoise　亀　60
　　［14］　Lake Shinji　宍道湖　64
　　［15］　About Kasuga at Matsue　松江の春日について　68
　　［16］　The Japanese Monkey　日本猿　76
　　［17］　The fashions of Old Japan Part I – The House
　　　　　古代日本の様式　そのI－住居　78
　　［18］　The fashions of Old Japan Part II – The Clothing
　　　　　古代日本の様式　そのII－衣服　84
　　［19］　To Mr. Lafcadio Hearn　ラフカディオ・ハーン先生へ　86
　　［20］　Fencing　剣道　90
　　［21］　About the Gymnastic Contest of Last Saturday
　　　　　先週土曜日の運動会について　94
　　［22］　The Centipede　百足　110
　　［23］　How did you spend this summer vacation?
　　　　　この夏休みをどう過ごしましたか？　112

- [24] The Owl　梟　118
- [25] About the little insects which fly to the lamps at night and burn themselves to death　夜、飛んで灯に入り焼け死ぬ小虫について　122
- [26] Composition: [An Autumn Walk]　作文：［秋の散策］　124

「田辺勝太郎」の英作文添削 ……………………………………………………… 131

- [27] Rice　米　132
- [28] The Seven Deities of Good Fortune　七福神　134
- [29] The Frog　蛙　136
- [30] The Most wonderful Thing　最も素晴らしいもの　140
- [31] Wrestling　相撲　144
- [32] Letter about Matsue to a friend　友への松江便り　148
- [33] Why should we venerate our Ancestors?　祖先を敬うべき理由は何か？　152
- [34] The fox who borrowed the Tiger's Power　虎の威を借る狐　156
- [35] The weather of the 15th January　1月15日の天候　160
- [36] The Tortoise　亀　162
- [37] The Japanese Spider　日本の蜘蛛　164
- [38] To a Bookseller asking for a book　書店に本を注文すること　168
- [39] To My Father　父へ　170
- [40] Tea　茶　172
- [41] The Owl　梟　176
- [42] About what I Dislike　私の嫌いなものについて　180
- [43] The Kite　鳶　182
- [44] The lotus　蓮　184
- [45] Lacquer ware　漆器　186
- [46] Fire-men　消防士　188
- [47] The Uguisu －(The name of a Japanese Singing-bird)　鶯－(日本の歌鳥の名前)　190
- [48] Composition: [Emperor]　作文：［天皇］　192
- [49] Swimming　水泳　194
- [50] To answer the question, "What are you going to do after you have finished your studies in the Chiugakkò?"　「中学校を卒業して貴方はどうするのか？」という問いに答えて　200

ハーンによる英作文添削の分類と分析 ……………………………………… 202

後記 ……………………………………………………………………………… 214

序　文

小泉　凡
島根県立大学

　1890年4月4日、ジャーナリストとして来日したラフカディオ・ハーン（小泉八雲／1850－1904）は、派遣元であるハーパー社との認識のずれからその契約を解消し、日本が大いに気に入ったこともあり、居住を決意した。まもなく、帝国大学のチェンバレンやニューオーリンズ時代にすでに面識をもっていた文部省の服部一三らの紹介で島根県尋常中学校と師範学校で英語教師の道を歩むことになった。8月30日に松江着、9月3日に初授業を行った。これが教師ハーンとしてのキャリアの始まりである。40歳の時だった。

　隻眼で不器用だったハーンは、新任教員としてはたしてうまくやっていけるのか、自分自身も学校側も懸念がなかったわけではないだろう。ところが、予想に反して、その授業ぶりは生徒を魅了し、瞬く間に生徒の心をつかむことに成功した。もちろんそれは西田千太郎教頭らの惜しみない協力の賜物でもあったが、ハーンの読書体験、異文化体験によって裏付けられた広大な知識を背景とした授業、さらに生徒一人一人に対するきめ細かい指導が効を奏したといえる。

　このほど、熊本大学の西川盛雄先生とローゼン・アラン先生の手によって上梓され、ハーンの松江時代の生徒である大谷正信・田辺勝太郎の答案への添削文は「きめ細かい個人指導」というハーンの教育者としてのスキルの特色を証明するとても興味深い資料である。ハーンの松江時代の教師像は、自身の作品である「英語教師の日記から」や教え子たちの回想から、その全貌がおぼろげながらみえていたが、このような貴重な一次資料の公開によってディテールが明かされることは、松江に住む人間にとって実に興味深く幸せなことである。

　正しい英文には惜しみなくほめ言葉を与え、ネイティヴ・スピーカーでない日本人が誤解しやすい使用法の誤りなどは、わかりやすく例をあげながら正していくという実に丁寧な添削である。中には生徒の英作文の数倍に及ぶ長さの講評を書き込んだものもある。たしかに現在に比べてクラスが少人数であり、教師も現代のように事務的雑用に忙殺されることなく教育に専念しやすい環境があったこと、また生徒側の学ぶ意欲の違いなど周囲の環境に恵まれていたこともあろう。しかし、ハーンは自ら教育の重要性を強く認識している人間だった。

　晩年の東京時代、時を惜しむあまりほとんどの来客・面会者を拒絶していたハーンが、大久保小学校の父兄懇談会に際して依頼された講演会の講師を引き受けた。そのこと自体、教育について強い信念をもつハーンの一面が垣間見える。テーマは「父兄の教育上における注意」で次のように述べている。

　「日本では先生ばかりに頼りすぎてしまって、家で教育するということは少ない。家庭教育ということは、子供の将来の発達のありさまに肝要なものであります。子供が将来、いかような性質を現して来るか、善い者になるか悪い者になるか、成功するか。不成功になるかということは、子供の小さいうちに両親の施すところのやり方いかんによるのであります。（中略）子供をみやる時間がない、暇がないということをしばしば聞くけれども、これはいかがわしいこと

であろうと思う。小学校の子供の復習をみるとか明日の下稽古をしてやるとかいうことは、そうたくさんの時間はいらない」(『へるん』26号所収)

　この指摘は、日本の現代社会における「甘えの構造」に起因すると思われる教師の過重負担の問題に大いに通じるものである。ハーンは学校で教師に習う前に、家庭で両親が読書することを教えるべきで、予習復習の手ほどきを手伝うのは家庭での責務という価値観をもっていたことがわかる。ハーン自身の子供時代はどうだったかといえば、両親からほとんど見放された状態で、大叔母のサラ・ブレナンが経済的な養育者となった。そしてすぐには学校にあげられず、家庭教師（チューター）によって在宅学習をしていたことは、アイルランド時代のハーンに関する詳細な評伝 *A Fantastic Journey* を上梓したポール・マレー氏が同書の中で、ヴァージニア大学バレット文庫にあるハーン自筆の自叙伝を引用しつつ紹介している。当時は、まだヨーロッパの上流階級の家庭では家庭教師教育が存在していたのだ。この家庭教師がハーンに妖精譚や怪談を語ったコナハト出身のキャサリン・コステロと同一人物かどうかは定かでないが、とにかく個人対個人によるきめ細かい指導を受け、その個人に適した指導、ひいてはその人の個性をのばす教育の意義を認識していたのではないだろうか。さらに、それは学校だけでなく、家庭で補完されるべきものと考えていたようだ。

　自らも長男一雄に対して、5歳になる少し前から英語を中心とした在宅教育を開始し、「私、大学で幾百人の書生に教えるよりも、ただ一人の一雄に教える方、何ほう難しいです」（小泉一雄「父八雲を憶う」）と時に苦しみ嘆息しながらも亡くなる直前までチューター教育を実践していたことはその証なのではないか。だから学校教育といえど、ひとりひとりの個性を見極め、それに適した指導をするということはハーンの信念であったのだろう。

　本書で明らかにされる、生徒の英作文と教師ハーンの添削文からは、両者の息使いが響いてくる。何よりハーンの教師としての個性を明らかにする一級の資料である。また、島根県尋常中学校の生徒に対してハーンはどんな課題を出し、どんな添削をしたのか、また当時の学生が何に関心をもち、どのような価値観をもっていたのかを知ることは、明治20年代の松江の文化資源の探究ということにもなる。

　ハーンの帝国大学時代でのちに英文学者・詩人として活躍する上田敏がハーンに提出したウィリアム・コリンズ論は、ハーンによってやはり丁寧な添削を受け、1930年に写真版で少部数発行されたという経緯もある。しかし、本書は翻刻・翻訳という大きな労力を要する作業の成果も付加されている点で、学術出版物としての価値を一層高めている。また、邦訳でも楽しく読むことができる点では、教育やハーンに関心のある多くの一般読者の方に一読いただきたい一冊でもある。編著者のご努力に松江に住む者として、また子孫の一人として心から感謝申し上げる。

（ハーン曾孫）

English Foreword

Though Lafcadio Hearn always considered his main vocation to be that of a writer, by all accounts he was also a most conscientious and inspiring teacher. At Matsue Middle School (1890-91), his first official teaching job, Hearn taught a variety of English language classes, and among them was English Composition, which he taught to 4th and 5th year students. These classes were especially interesting to him in that his students' writing gave him valuable first-hand information about Japanese culture and even more valuable insight into their young Japanese minds and hearts. Every week, or nearly so, he assigned his boys a fresh topic to contemplate and write about in English, and every week he diligently read and corrected their efforts. The errors he corrected were mostly in grammar, spelling, and mechanics, rectified with a cross-out and a word or two written above the lines, but sometimes he gave detailed explanations or made suggestions for modifying content.

Fortunately, about 90 pages of these compositions, written by Otani Masanobu and Tanabe Katsutaro and corrected by Hearn, were recently discovered in the Kumamoto Prefectural Library, Kumamoto, Japan, preserved in the form of glass plates, apparently in preparation for a publication that somehow never happened. These plates provide precious new examples of Hearn's mind at work. From them we can learn more about the style and content of Hearn's teaching, his relationship with his students, and the development of his interest in and knowledge about a variety of topics concerning Japan. Professor Morio Nishikawa and I are pleased to be able to reproduce all of the extant original manuscripts alongside a transcription of each into typeface that clearly indicates exactly what Hearn added or modified to improve the work of his students. To make the material more accessible to Japanese who may have difficulty with the content, Professor Nishikawa has provided a Japanese translation of each composition and an introductory essay on the significance of the materials.

Although every effort was made to make our transcriptions as accurate as possible, in a few places we were unable to establish whether an over-write was made by Hearn or by the student himself during the process of composition. In other places, the writing was simply illegible to us. These places have been noted accordingly. If the reader should recognize any omissions or errors in our transcriptions, we would be grateful for notification.

Alan Rosen

経緯と解説

　ラフカディオ・ハーン（小泉八雲）はアメリカではシンシナティで8年、ニューオーリンズで10年、その後当時のフランス領西インド諸島のマルティニク島で2年、計20年の長きにわたって有能なジャーナリストとして活躍していた。その後ニューヨークのハーパー社の企画にのって来日した。その主旨は日本取材によるルポルタージュ記事の作成であったが、ハーパー社とハーンの行き違いからからこの計画は頓挫する。

　ハーンは明治23年（1890）松江の島根県尋常中学校と師範学校で英語教員としての仕事に就くが、その時も日本に関わる彼の姿勢はどこまでもジャーナリスト的であり、日本を「取材して、書いて、伝える」という姿勢に貫かれていた。

　来日に際して『ハーパーズ・マンスリー』社の美術主任であったウィリアム・パットンに提出した企画書の文面をみると日本滞在中の取材予定項目がきめ細かく記されている。以後ハーンの日本滞在の仕事の目標はこの項目に沿って調べ、取材して書き、これを西洋に向けて発信するという作業を持続することになる。企画書の内容の骨子は田部隆次著『小泉八雲』（p.89）により、以下の通り記しておきたい。

　　「第一印象、気候と風景、日本の自然の詩的分子」
　　「外国人にとっての都市生活」
　　「日常生活における美術、美術品に対する外国影響の結果」
　　「新文化」「娯楽」「芸者およびその職業」
　　「新教育制度—子どもの生活—子どもの遊戯等」
　　「家庭生活と一般家庭の宗教」
　　「公の祭祀法、—寺院の儀式と礼拝者のつとめ」
　　「珍しき伝説と迷信」「日本の婦人生活」　「古い民謡と歌」
　　「芸術界における—日本の古い大家、生き残ってあるいは記憶となって与えている感化、日本
　　　の自然と人生の反映者としての勢力」
　　「珍しき一般の言語、—日常生活における奇異な言葉の習慣」
　　「社会的組織、—政治上および軍事上の状態」
　　「移住地としての日本、外国分子の地位等」

　これらの項目への関心はハーンが教員になってからも基本的に変わることはなかった。ハーンは来日後明治23年（1890）9月から明治24年（1891）10月まで松江で教壇に立ち、その後明治24年11月より明治27年（1894）10月までの3年間弱、熊本の第五高等中学校の教壇に立っている。その間日本人の生活、文化、宗教などに深い関心を寄せ、学校では生徒に英作文の課題を出し、日本

島根県尋常中学校（『教育者ラフカディオ・ハーンの世界』より）

のことを書かせ、その英文添削を行った。それは生徒にとっては英語力向上の契機となり、ハーンにとっては日本事情を理解するための取材の一環として格好のものとなった。

このハーン先生による英作文添削のガラス乾板は故木下順二氏を介して熊本に送られ、これを熊本県立図書館（熊本近代文学館併設）が長らく保管していた。これがハーン没後100年の平成16年（2004）6月にその存在が明らかになり、すでに新聞などで報道されたところであった。

このガラス乾板はハーンの松江時代の教え子である大谷正信と田辺勝太郎のものであった。この二人についての略歴は概略以下の通りである。

■大谷正信　［明治8年（1875）―昭和8年（1933）］

大谷正信は明治8年松江市殿町に生まれ、旧制松江中学時代の3年生から4年生のはじめにかけてハーンの英語の授業を受けている。松江中学を田辺勝太郎よりも一年遅く明治25年（1892）7月に第12期生として卒業している。英文学者、俳人で大谷繞石と称した。松江中学の後、京都の第三高等中学校に進学した。ここで高浜虚子や河東碧梧桐と出会い俳句を始めた。明治27年に仙台の第二高等学校に転学、その後帝国大学文科大学に入学。ここで子規庵の正岡子規と知り合う。ここでも帝国大学に赴任して来ていたハーン先生の授業を再び受けることになる。この年の12月からハーンの日本研究の助手を頼まれ、ハーンの作品構成のための日本についての資料を多く提供する。明治32年（1899）に帝国大学を卒業。後には第四高等学校の教授となりイギリスにも留学。晩年は広島高等師範学校の教授となった。なおハーンが松江から熊本に行くに際して生徒を代表して送辞を述べたのは彼であった。

■田辺勝太郎　［明治5年（1872）―昭和6年（1931）］

田辺勝太郎は明治5年2月に島根県仁多郡三村の金坂家の三男として生まれ、幼時に飯石郡吉田村田辺家の嗣子となった。松江中学を明治24年7月に第11期生として卒業している。その後暫らく小学校で教鞭をとったがすぐに仙台の第二高等学校に入学。次いで東京帝国大学工科大学採鉱冶金科に学んで明治31年（1898）卒業後古河鉱業に聘せられて以後日本各地の採鉱冶金鉱業の領

（写真〈左〉）ハーンと大谷正信
（写真〈右〉）島根県尋常中学校記念写真（明治24年撮影）の田辺勝太郎（前列一番左）。後列右がハーン

域で活躍し、院内銀山(秋田県)、足尾銅山(栃木県)を経て西部(福岡県)古河鉱業所長から取締役となって日本の採鉱冶金工業の領域で大きな足跡を残した。昭和2年(1927)にはアルミニウム合金を発見して学位を取り精力的な日々を送った。晩年は和歌、書画・骨董などを嗜む豊かな趣味人として生き、昭和6年1月に逝去している。ハーンは明治24年(1891)11月30日付の田辺に宛てた手紙で「Your Old Teacher」という言い方で心のこもった気持を伝え、田辺の書いた作文に触れて英語の勉強を怠らないようにと述べている。

　このガラス乾板に見る英作文とハーン先生による添削はすべて手書きである。そのため内容の正確な①判読、②復元、③日本語訳の作業が必須となった。この作業が日本学術振興会の科学研究費補助金（基盤研究（C)、課題番号18520438)の支援により成り、熊本県立図書館(近代文学館併設)に報告することができた。その意義は「文学者ハーン」という側面だけではなく「教育者ハーン」の実像を理解する上で貴重な資料となるものと思われる。

　次にこのガラス乾板についての事実関係について以下に整理しておきたい。
- ガラス乾板は熊本県立図書館に所属・保管されている
- ページの割り振り、行数、文字数、文字位置は原板通りにした
- 生徒の書体は普通体、ハーン先生の訂正とコメントは斜体(イタリック)にして識別できるようにした
- 部分的な活字初出は「明治37年12月17日識」として英語青年（Vol. XII, No. 12: pp. 230-31)に「Lafcadio Hearn 氏の英文添削実例」と題して大谷正信が本人のものについて一枚のみ執筆紹介している
- 当該生徒は旧制松江中学(島根県尋常中学校)の生徒であった大谷正信と田辺勝太郎である

　ハーンのコメントのポイントは基本的な英語の誤りの指摘とその訂正に加えて生徒への励ましがあり、教育者としての目線は低く、生徒たちに寄り添っている姿がよく窺える。また語源を知ることの大切さを指摘し、コメントの中でもハーン自身ハーバート・スペンサーの影響を受けていることに鑑みて、当時の日本国について適者生存の原理の観点から生徒たちの蒙を啓くようなコメントを随所で行っている。また若者には礼儀の大切さを述べ、文明や宗教の問題にも触れて教育者としての優れた見識を示したものとなっている。

　基礎資料であるガラス乾板は原物そのものではない。原物の一部は京都外国語大学附属図書館に十数枚存在していることは分かっているが、同大学からの学術的研究報告はまだ聞かない。他の原物の所在場所は不明である。恐らくは先の戦災で焼失したか散逸したものと思われる。活字になったものとしては上記大谷正信の記事の次は東京大学教授市河三喜博士の編纂に関わる『サム・ニュー・レターズ・ライティングズ』(大正4年(1923)刊)のpp. 374-79にハーンの2課題分と原物の写真一枚が掲載されていることをここに記しておく。

経緯と解説　　9

判読と復元の手続き

　これは2004年6月に熊本県立図書館において見つかったラフカディオ・ハーンによる学生の書いた英作文添削テキスト二人分の判読とその忠実な復元作業の結果報告とその邦訳である。この添削は島根県尋常中学校でハーン先生の英作文の授業を受けた学生のうち、大谷正信と田辺勝太郎の分である。
　構成は⑴ガラス乾板に見られるオリジナルテキストの写真複製、⑵そのテキストの判読と復元結果、⑶テキスト内容の日本語翻訳、の三部から構成されている。

⑴は上記二学生の英文とハーン先生の添削によるオリジナルなハンド・ライティングのガラス乾板からの写真複製である
⑵は⑴の復元結果である。テキストがすべてハンド・ライティングであるため判読し難い箇所があったが、それはそのままにして主観的な予測・推測は排した
⑶は大意を取るためになるべく自然な日本語に訳出した

　なお⑵において判読・復元の方法・手続きとしては以下の通り統一した。

①誤り・訂正の箇所は書かれた語や句(文)の上から削除の印として棒線(―――)、または斜線(＼や／)を引いた
②上記棒線箇所の訂正に際してはテキストに従い記号(∧)を挿入し、その上にハーン先生の新たな訂正結果をイタリック体で明示した
③ハーン先生が訂正された語句はすべてイタリック体で示した
④ハーン先生による直接の長めのコメント(時にページ全体にわたる)の箇所もイタリック体で示した
⑤訂正箇所が語の一部を生かす形のものでハーン先生によって新たに付加・修正されたものは＜　＞を用いて中の語句をイタリック体にした
　　(例　＜*the*＞, w＜*ere*＞, east＜*ern*＞, sa＜*p*＞phire, borrows＜*ed*＞)

　なお訳出に際して、タイトルの次に来て右端に学年を表す序数があるが、この表記法は学年(year)と組または級(class)の二種類あるが、"th"のみの場合は「学年」の方で統一した。また、目次の［　］付きのタイトルは作文(Composition)と記されているのみゆえに、本文中のタイトル相当の語句をとってタイトルとした。

判読・復元・日本語訳

「大谷正信」の英作文添削

The Compositions of Ōtani Masanobu

[1] The Hototogisu　ホトトギス

Composition.
　　　4th　M. Otani's

The Hototogisu.

I do not know ~~some~~ any particular facts about the Hototogisu. ~~His~~ voice is strong, and clear. ~~His~~ other name is ~~Kuwacko~~ Quackō (クヮッコ)* and it comes from ~~its~~ voice, and its pronunci~~ing~~ation resembles the "wood cuckoo". The best time to hear ~~him~~ it is in the stillness of a moonlight night. In Japan, there are many poems about the Hototogisu. I will write down one of the famous poems. "Hototogisu nakitsuru kata o nagamure-ba ~~tata~~ tada ariake no tsuki zo nokoreru". It means that "when you will look ~~at~~ in the direction[2] in which Hototogisu cried, there remains only a obscure ("dim" would be better) morning moon". The Hototogisu is not said to sing, but to cry or to vomit ~~the~~ blood. There is another poem. "Hototogisu chini naku koe wa ariake no tsuki yori hokani

---
* In Romaji, write "Kw" instead of "Quw." Better to say — Kwakko.　[2] You cannot look at a direction, — because a direction is not a thing.

Composition.

    4th M. Otani

The Hototogisu.

     any
I do not know ~~some~~ particular facts
about the Hototogisu. ~~His~~ <*Its*> voice
is strong, and clear. ~~His~~ <*Its*> other
name is ~~Kuwwackō~~ ,+ Quackō (郭公)
and it comes from ~~his~~ <*its*> voice, and
     ation   *word*
its pronouncing ∧ resembles ~~to~~ the ∧ cuckoo.
     it
The best time to hear ~~him~~ is in the
stillness of a moonlight night.
In Japan, there are many poems
about the Hototogisu. I will
    the
write down one of ∧ famous poems.
"Hototogisu nakitsuru kata o nagamure
-ba ~~tada~~ tada ariakeno tsukizo
nokoreru." It means that "when you
    in the
will look ~~at~~ ∧ direction(2) in which Hototogisu cried, there remains only a
  "dim" would be better
obscure morning moon." The Hototogisu
is not said to sing, but to cry or
to vomit ~~the~~ blood. There is another
poem. Hototogisu chini naku koe
wa ariake no tsuki yori hokani

―――

* In Romaji – write "Kw" instead of "Quw." Better to
 say – Kwakko. (2) You cannot look at a direction, –
 because a direction is not a thing.

作文

    4年 大谷　M.

ホトトギス

私はホトトギスについてはほとんど何も知らない。その声は力強くはっきりと聞え、別名は郭公である。それは鳴き声がcuckooという語に似て発せられるところから来ている。その声を聞くには月夜の静かな晩が最もよい。日本ではホトトギスを歌った歌が多くある。有名なものでは「ホトトギス鳴きつる方をながむればただ有明の月ぞのこれる」をここに記しておこう。それは「ホトトギスが鳴いている方角を見るとただ朧な有明の月の残像が見えている」というほどの意味である。ホトトギスは歌うのではなくて叫ぶ、あるいは血を吐くのだと言われている。詩がもう一つある。「ホトトギス血になく声は有明の月より他に

―――

* ローマ字では"Quw"ではなく"Kw"と書きなさい。"Kwakko"と言う方が良い。
(2) 方向 (direction) はものではないので direction を見る (look) ことは出来ない。

[1] The Hototogisu ホトトギス 13

kiku hito mo nashi. It means that, "Except a morning moon, there is no hearer of the cry which Hototogisu made when it vomited the blood."

"Blood"; "water"; "wine"; "oil" do not need any definite article except when particularized.

You might say: "The blood of the camel is different from that of all other animals, because its corpuscles are elliptical [⬭] instead of round [○]"

But again we have the proverb:— "Blood is thicker than water." Here, you see, there is no article;— "blood" and "water" being simply names of substances, like element in chemistry, which need no article.

kiku hito mo nashi. It means that, "except a morning moon, there is no hearer ~~on~~ <of> the cry which Hoto-togisu ∧ vomited ~~the~~ blood."

☞ "Blood"; "water"; "wine"; "oil" do not need any definite article <u>except</u> when particularized.
You might say: "<u>The</u> blood of the camel is different from that of all other animals, because its corpuscles are elliptical [🫘] instead of round [⬤]"
But again we have the proverb:— "Blood is thicker than water." Here, you see, there is no article;— "blood" and "water" being simply names of substances, like elements in chemistry, which need no article.

聞く人もなし」。これは「ホトトギスは血を吐くまでも鳴くというのにその声を聞くのは有明の月だけである」という意味である。

「血」「水」「葡萄酒」「油」といった語は特定化する場合以外定冠詞は取らない。「駱駝の血液 (<u>The</u> blood of the camel) の血球は丸型 [⬤] ではなく丸の欠けた型 [🫘] であるがゆえに他の動物の血液とは違っている」といった言い方は確かにできる。
しかし「血は水よりも濃し (Blood is thicker than water.)」のような諺の例がある。ここで注意すべきことは、「血」や「水」は物質の名前でしかなく、化学物質の元素と同様冠詞をとることはない、ということである。

[1] The Hototogisu ホトトギス 15

【2】The Greatest Japanese　最も偉大な日本人

Composition
　　　　4th. Class.
　　　　　M. Ōtani

The Greatest Japanese.

Mr. T. Saigō, K. Kido, and T. Ōkubo were called the three great men of Japan. When I read the biographys of these men, I thought Mr. T. Ōkubo was the greatest. His native country was Satsuma. His character was very different from that of other boys as a child. In play he became always the head of all the other boys. After many efforts he overthrew the feudal system of the Tokugawas, and established the present government.

　　　(to be continued)

　　　　　Very good

Composition

    4th Class
    M. Ōtani

 The Greatest Japanese.

 Mr. T. Saigō, K. Kido, and T. Ōkubo
were called ∧ *the* three great men ~~in~~ <*of*> Japan.
When I read the biographys of
these men, I thought Mr. T. Ōkubo
~~is~~ *was the* ∧ greatest. His native country ~~is~~
was Satsuma. His character
was very different from that of other
boys as a child. In play he
became always the head of all <*the*>
       efforts
other boys. After many ~~matters~~
 epis
~~and cases~~, he overthrew the feudal
system of <*the*> Tokugawa*s*, and established
the
∧ present government.
    (to be continued)

    Very good

作文

    4組
    大谷　M.
最も偉大な日本人

 西郷、木戸、大久保は日本の三偉人と言われてきた。これらの偉人の伝記を読んでみると、私は大久保が一番偉いと思った。彼の生れは薩摩の国である。性格は子供の時から他の子供たちとは大いに違っていた。遊んでいても彼はいつも他の子供たちの大将であった。彼はいろいろ苦労した挙句に徳川封建制度を倒して現在の政府を樹立したのである。
   （続く）

   とても良くできました

【3】The greatest Japanese Part II　最も偉大な日本人 そのII

Composition.
　　　　　　4th M. Ōtani
The greatest Japanese.
　Part II.

Mr. T. Okubo advised ~~to~~ our emperor to change ~~to Tōkio~~ his capital to its ^(situation,) present ~~,~~ Tōkio. Indeed, it was quite necessary to do so. He went to China as ~~the~~ ^(minister) ~~residency~~, and he ~~entreated~~ ^(negotiated) ^(successfully) ~~eloquently to~~ ^(with the) ~~many~~ ministers of China for the affair of Formosa island, ~~which was~~ ^(showing) very remarkable ^(power) ~~diplomatic~~. The Chin~~ese~~ ^(affair) empire paid for that ~~effort~~ ^(affair) 600 thousand pound (?) as ~~"~~ ^("an indemnity" is better) ~~compensation~~ of the war ^(and the cost of) ~~that~~ our expedition ~~for battled with the natives~~ of ^(to) that island. He was slain by a villain who was called I. Shimada in the city of Tōkio. ~~Alas!~~

The word "Resident", — (not "residency") is a word meaning the representative of a government in a subject country, or colony, — as in British India. I think you mean "ambassador" or "minister plenipotentiary."

Composition.
             4th M. Ōtani

The greatest Japanese.
      Part II.

Mr. T. Ōkubo advised ~~to~~ our emperor
                     his
to change ~~to Tōkio~~ ∧capital to its
situation, ──
present ∧Tōkio.   Indeed, it was
quite necessary to do so.   He
                    minister
went to China as ~~the residency,~~
         negotiated successfully
and he ~~entreated eloquently to~~
with the
~~many~~ ministers of China for
the affair of Formosa island,
           showing   *powers*
~~which was~~ ∧very remarkable *diplomatic* ∧.
The
  ∧Chin~~a~~ <*ese*> empire paid for that
         affair
~~effect~~ ∧ 600 thousand pound (?)
   "an indemnity" is better
as compensation <*for*> ~~of~~ the war.
    and the cost of
~~that~~ ∧ our expedition ~~battled~~
~~with the natives of~~ <*to*> that island.
He was slain by a villain
who was called I. Shimada
in the city of Tōkio. Alas!

The word "Resident", −(not "residency") is
a word meaning the representative of a government
in a <u>subject</u> country, or colony, −as in
British India. I think you mean "ambassador"
or "minister plenipotentiary."

作文
           4年 大谷 M.
最も偉大な日本人
　　そのII

大久保氏は天皇に首都を現在の東京に遷都することをご進言申し上げた。まことそうする必要があったのだ。彼は大臣として中国に行き、中国閣僚との交渉に成功した。台湾問題ではすぐれた外交能力を発揮し、戦争賠償金とこの島への遠征費として中国（清）の皇帝は60万ポンド（？）支払った。そして彼は島田という暴漢に東京で殺害された。あー！

"Resident"という語は―("residency"ではありません)<u>属国</u>あるいは英国の場合のように植民地政府の代表を意味する語です。君は「<u>大使</u>」あるいは「<u>全権公使</u>」のことを言っているだと思うのだが。

【4】The fire-fly 蛍

Composition. —
  4th M. Ōtani

The fire-fly.

The fire-fly is a small insect, which only appears ~~in the~~ during summer nights. It ~~has~~ ~~the~~ a red head and black wings, and its tail is made ~~of~~ so as to twinkle like little stars. Its Japanese name is hotaru. I think, the word hotaru came from hi-taru which means "fire-drop". In ~~Old~~ ancient old China, there ~~had been~~ once lived a very diligent student who was very poor, and could not buy ~~the~~ a candle or oil to light. He was accustomed to read his book ~~in the~~ on summer nights by the aid of ~~the~~ a strange lamp, which ~~is~~ was ~~the~~ myriads of ~~this~~ were enclosed insects. So, in Japan, any man who works very very zealously, is said "to work

Composition.

     4th M. Ōtani

The fire-fly.

The fire-fly is a small insect,
which only appears ~~in the~~ *during* summer
nights. It ha~~ve~~ <s> ~~the~~ <a> red head and
black wings, and its tail is made
~~of~~ *so* as to twinkle like little
stars. Its Japanese name is
<u>hotaru</u>. I think, the word <u>hotaru</u>
came from <u>hi</u>-<u>taru</u> which means
"fire-drop." In ~~Old old~~ *ancient* China,
there ~~had been~~ *once lived* a very diligent
student who was very poor, and
could not buy ~~the~~ *a* candle or
oil to *give him* light. He was accustomed to read his book ~~in the~~ <on>
summer nights by the aid of ~~the~~
a strange lamp <in> which ~~is the~~
were enclosed
myriads of ~~this~~ <these> insects. So, in
Japan, any man who work<s> very
very zealously, is said "to work

作文

     4年 大谷 M.

蛍

蛍は夏の夜だけに現れる小さな昆虫です。頭は赤く、羽は黒く、お尻には星のようにピカリと小さく光ります。その日本名は<u>蛍</u>ですが、<u>蛍</u>という語は「火の雫」を表す<u>火垂る</u>から来ていると思われます。古代中国では、とても貧しく蝋燭や灯を点すための油を買うことのできない勤勉な生徒がいました。彼は夏の夜はこの虫の発するたくさんの光のおかげで書物を読んでいました。そこで日本では熱心によく勉強する人は「蛍の光で

by fire-fly-light. Every boys very much likes to pursue and catch it. We may often hear some boy who loudly speaks (sings?) while pursuing it. these words:— "Hotāru koè midzu nomashō, āchi no midzu wa nigaizo, kōchi no midzu wa āmaizo." It means, "Come here, fire-fly! I will give you some water. Yonder water is bitter and this place's water is very sweet!" It is used as medicine by some doctors.

by fire-fly =*light*. Every boys very <*much*>
likes to pursue and catch it.

We ~~can~~ *may often* hear some boy who loudly
speaks ✗ ⟨sings ?⟩ *while pursuing it* ~~at the time of~~
~~pursuit.~~ ~~It is such~~ <these> word*s* :— "Hotaru
~~coe~~<koi> midzu nomashō, āchi no
midzu wa nigaizo, kōchi no
midzu wa āmaizo." It
means ~~that~~, "Come here, fire-fly!
I will ~~furnish the~~ *give you some* ∧ water ~~to you~~.
Yonder water is bitter and
this place's water is very sweet!"

It is used ~~some~~ *as* ∧ medicine by
some doctors.

勉強する」という言い方をします。男の子は皆蛍を追いかけて捕まえることが好きです。蛍を追っかけている時子供が大声で「ほたる来い、水のましょー。あーちの水はにーがいぞ、こーちの水はあーまいぞ」というのが聞こえます。その言葉は、「蛍さん、こっちにおいで！水をあげましょう。あっちの水はにがいよ。こっちの水はとても甘いよ。」という意味です。蛍を薬として使う医者もいます。

[4] The fire-fly 蛍

【5】The mountain called Dai-sen　大山と呼ばれる山

Composition.
4th. M. Otani

The mountain called Dai-sen.

The mountain called Dai-sen is a high extinct volcano and it is twenty miles away off from Matsue. The top of that mountain is always covered with white snow except during a few months in the summer. It resembles mount Fuji which is the highest peak in Japan, and it is the best view of it that to be had from our country, therefore it is called generally the Idzumo-Fuji. On that mountain there are many Buddhist temples, because that place is very quiet and therefore it favourable meditation upon the sacred and the inviolable doctrine.

Very good

Composition.

        4th. M. Ōtani

The mountain called
    Dai-sen.

The mountain called Dai-sen is a high extinct volcano and it is twenty miles ~~off~~ *away* from Matsue. The top of that mountain is always covered with ~~the~~ white snow except ∧ *during a* few months in the summer. It resembles ~~to~~ mount.Fuji which is the highest peak in Japan, and ~~it is~~ <*the*> best view ~~to look~~ *of it is that to be had* ∧ from our country, therefore it is called generally the Idzumo-Fuji. On that mountain there are many Buddhist temples, because that place is very quiet and ∧ *is therefore* ~~enable~~ ∧ ~~####~~ *favourable* to ~~muse~~ ∧ *meditation upon* the sacred and the inviolable doctrine.

        Very good

作文

        4年　大谷　M.

大山と
呼ばれる山

大山という山は標高の高い死火山で松江から20マイル離れたところにあります。山頂は夏の2、3ヶ月を除いていつも雪で覆われています。形は日本一高い富士山に似ています。私たちの所からの眺めが一番いいので一般には出雲富士と言われます。山の上は静かで、神聖にして揺ぐことのない教えについて瞑想できるものですから多くの仏教寺院があります。

        とてもよく出来ました

【6】The Botan　牡丹

Composition.
　　　　　　4th M. Otani

The Botan.

　The Botan is sometimes called Hatsuka-so which means "the grass that blooms during twenty days long." Its scientific name is Paeonia Montan. Its root is used as medicine. There are many thousand species of Botan, and the colors of their flowers are very different — bright red, red, blue, green, white, etc. The Botan is sometimes compared to the agreeable [a charming (or pretty)] woman. There is a proverb about the Botan. When a beautiful woman stands, she is the herbaceous peony (Shaken-yaku), and when she sits, she is the Botan, and when she walks, her appearance much resembles the lily (Yu-ri). Some man says that the Botan is the queen of all

(1) "Agreeable" refers to manners — not to appearance.

Compositan. *io*

4ᵗʰ M. Ōtani

The Botan.

The Botan is sometimes called Hatsuka-so which means "the grass that blooms during twenty days long." Its scientific name is Paeonia Montan. ~~funs~~ Its root is used as medicine. There are many thousand species of Botan, and the colors of ~~its every~~ *their* flowers, are very different —— bright red, red, blue, green [?], white, etc. The Botan is sometimes compared to the ~~agreable~~ *a charming (or pretty)* ⁽¹⁾ woman. There ~~are~~ is a proverb about the Botan. When *a beautiful woman she* ~~it~~ stands, ~~it~~ is the herbaceous peony (Shaku-yaku), and when ~~it~~ <she> sits, ~~it~~ <she> is the Botan, and when ~~it~~ *she* walks, ~~its~~ *her* appearance ~~is~~ very *much* resembles the lily (Yu-ri). Some man says that the Botan is the queen of all

(1) "Agreeable" refers to manners – not to appearance.

作文

4年　大谷 M.

牡丹

牡丹は、「二十日間だけ咲く草」ということで時に二十日草といわれます。その学問的名称は Paeonia Montan で、その根は薬として使われます。牡丹には何千という種類があり、その花の色は明るい赤、赤、青、緑 [?]、白などとさまざまに異なっています。牡丹は時に美しい女性に喩えられます。牡丹については「立てば芍薬、座れば牡丹、歩く姿は百合の花」という俚諺がある。人々の中には「牡丹は」花の女王だという人がいるくらいです。

(1) "agreeable" はマナーについて云うもので ~~容姿~~ について云うことはない。

[6]　The Botan　牡丹　　27

flowers, but I think the Botan has no ✗ sweet smell. So it is inferior ~~than~~ to the Sakura (the cherry flower?) which is compared to Yamato gokoro of Shikishima (means "the spirit of the Japanese"). There is a island which is called ✗ Daikon shima, 4 or 5 miles ~~far away~~ distant from Matsue in the direction of the east. Every houses of that island has a garden in them many beautiful Botan plants.

flowers, but I think the Botan has no ~~l~~ sweet smell. So it is inferior ~~than~~ *to* the Sakura (the cherry flower?) which is compared to Yamato gokoro of Shikishima (means "the spirit of ∧*the* Japanese"). There is a island which is called ~~P~~ Daikon shima, 4 or 5 miles *distant* ~~far away~~ from Matsue in the direction of ∧*the* east. Every houses of that island ~~have~~ <has> ∧*a garden with* many beautiful Botan <plants>.

しかし、牡丹はあまりいい香りがしないと思う。そして敷島の大和心（これは日本人の精神を表します。）に喩えられる桜よりも劣っています。松江から東の方4または5マイル離れたところに大根島と呼ばれる島があります。この島のどの家にも美しい牡丹がたくさん咲いている庭があります。

Hina matsuri 雛祭り

Composition.

5th M. Otani

Hina matsuri.

The Sekku of March is the third day of that month, and it is the feast days of girls. That the festival of Sekku came from China, is certainty. The other name of the Hinamatsuri is Hina asobi. From 28th day or 29th day of February, every ~~house~~ family who have the girls make the shelves or stairs a series of shelves, estrades and put on the images of the Emperor, empress and eminent warriors of old Japan upon them. It is said that the festival of Hinamatsuri commenced ~~began~~ from the second year of the Emperor Bitatsu. In that time, the Hina was made of paper. Some man says it has the same meaning as ~~with~~ the paper man-shape which is used

Composition.

5th M. Ōtani

Hina matsuri.

The Sekku of March is *the* third day of that month, and it is the feast day of girls. That the festival of Sekku came from China, is certain~~ly~~. The ~~oh~~ other name of <the> Hinamatsuri is Hina asobi. From 28th day or 29th day of February, every ~~house~~ *family* who have ~~the~~ girls make ~~the~~ shelf<ves> or ~~stair a series of shelves~~, *estrades* and put ~~on~~ the images of the Emperor, empress and eminent warriors of Old Japan *upon them*. It is said that the festival of Hinamatsuri ~~began~~ *commenced* from the second year of the Emperor Bitatsu. In that time, <the> Hina was made of paper. Some man says it has the same meaning ~~with~~ *as* the paper man-shape which is used

作文

5年　大谷 M.

雛祭り

3月の節句はその月の3日で女の子のお祭です。この節句を祝うことは中国から入ってきたことは間違いありません。雛祭りの別名は雛遊びです。2月28日か29日から女の子のいるどこの家でも棚や階段を作ってそこに天皇、皇后、昔の高貴な武人たちの人形を並べます。雛祭りのお祝いは敏達天皇の2年目から始まったとされています。当時雛は紙で作られていました。6月か12月の終わりに使われる紙の人形と同じ意味をもっているという人もいます。

at the ends of June or December. It means to transfer the uncleanness of our bodies to this man-shape, and to purify ourselves. It was the old customs to offer Mochi (A kind of bread made of rice) which is mixed with the plant called Yomogi (Artemisia?), to offer the white-wine and the wine which is made from the peach flowers, and to offer the toasted peas. On this day, cockfights were held at the court of Japan, in very ancient times.

at the end of June ~~and~~ *or* December. It means to transfer the unclean~~nesses~~ <ies> of our bod~~y~~ ~~and to purify ourselves~~ to this man-shape, and to purify our selves. It was *the* old customs to offer ~~the~~ mochi (A kind of bread made of rice) which is mixed with the ~~plad~~ plant called Yomogi (Artemisia?), to offer the white-wine and the wine which is made from the peach flowers, and to offer the toasted peas. I<O>n this day, ~~the fighting of cocks was~~ *cockfights were held* ~~practiced in~~ <at> the court of Japan, in very ancient times!

そのもつ意味は、肉体の不浄さを人形に乗り移らせ、自らの自我を浄化させることです。よもぎ(Artemisia?)という草の入ったもち(米でできたパンの一種)と、桃の花で作られた白い葡萄酒と炒った豆を供えるのが古い習慣でした。この日に古代日本の宮廷では闘鶏が行われました！

[7] Hina matsuri 雛祭り　33

Composition.

4. M. Ōtani

We must not compose long composition, I know. But to-day's subject of composition is very important and very interesting. So I am compelled to compose a long one. Please, pardon me.

What is the most awful thing? (My opinion might be very incorrect.) I think, the most awful thing in the present condition of Japan is the European, in particular the Christian. The nature of the European is very widely different from that of the Japanese[(1)]. Europeans do not know anything about the <u>Kōkō</u> 孝 which is translated into English as "obedience to parents" or "filial piety", (but it is not an exact translation in meaning,) and which is the first one of the five great foundations of Japanese morality. I have heard that when the parents and wife fell into the water

[(1)] After "different" always use "from".

Composition.

                4. M. Ōtani

We must not compose long composition, I know. But to-day's subject of composition is very important and very interest-ing. So I am compelled to compose a long one. Please, pardon me.

      What is the most awful thing?

(My opinion ~~will~~ *might* be very incorrect.) I think, the most awful thing in the present condition of Japan is the European, in particular the Christian. The nature of the European is very widely different ~~to~~ *from that of* the Japanese.[1] ~~The~~ Europeans do not know anything about the K̲ō̲k̲ō̲ 孝 which is translated into English as ~~the~~ "obedience to parents" or "filial piety," (but it is not ~~complete~~ *an exact* translation in ~~the~~ meaning,) and which is the first one of the five great foundations of Japanese morality. I have heard that when ~~the~~ parents and wife fall <in>to the water

  (1) *After "different" always use "f̲r̲o̲m̲."*

"At" "precise time"

~~the European will rescue his wife at first.~~ at the same time, the European will rescue his wife ~~at~~ first. But it is very absurd in Japanese morality. The Europeans feel no pain to leave their master and country, and have not so much fidelity, allegiance as Japanese. Therefore, in Europe there are many different lines of ~~the~~ Emperor, in the same country. But, in Japan there has always been ~~is~~ only one sacred ~~Emperor~~ families of Emperors ~~castle~~. A Christian said to me. There is no respectable thing in the world except God. — "He was a fool." — But in Japan there is a very sacred and most respectable person, ^His Majesty, who is called ~~the~~ a living statue by some Christians. (Only vulgar people) Some Christian says, that before ~~to~~ the photograph of Japanese Emperor, we should ~~need~~ not ~~to~~ blut our heads]* Such a man is not a true Japanese. Therefore a Christian ideas are ~~is~~ very injurious to the res-

* Such a man is a hypocrite and an ignoramus. In his own country, he would not dare to enter the room of one of Her Majesty's Consuls without taking off his hat. And a

"*At*" — *precise time*

~~the European will rescue his wife at first.~~
~~on~~ <*at*> the same time, the European will rescue his wife ~~at~~ first. But it is very absurd in Japanese morality. The Europeans feel no pain to leave their master and country, and have not so much fidelity, allegiance as Japanese. Therefore, in Europe there are many different lines of ~~the~~ Emperors in the same country. But, in Japan there
has always been   family of Emperors
is ∧ only one sacred ~~Emperor caste~~. A Christian said to me. There is no respectable thing in the world except God.

——— *"He was a fool."* ———
But in Japan there is a very secred and
           person,—
most respectable ∧ His Majesty, who is
        a
called ~~the~~ ∧ living statue by some Christians
   (only vulgar people)   that before
tians ∧. Some Christian says, ~~to~~ the photo-
                    should
graph of Japanese Emperor, we ~~need~~
not ~~to~~ bend our heads.* Such a man is not a true Japanese. Therefore
        ideas are
Christian ∧ ~~is~~ very injurious to the res-

*Such a man is a hypocrite and an ignoramus. In his own country, he would not dare to enter the room of one of Her Majesty's Consuls, without taking off his hat.

"*At*" ―正確な時を表す

ヨーロッパ人はまず妻を救うそうです。しかし日本の道徳ではこれは理に合いません。ヨーロッパ人は日本人のように自分の主人や国を離れるのに痛みを感じない。忠誠心や忠義心も大してもってはいない。従ってヨーロッパではさまざまな種類の皇帝の家系が出現した。しかし日本では唯一神聖な天皇家が古代から存在してきている。クリスチャンはこの世で神以外に敬すべきものはないと私に言った。
　　―「その人は愚か者だ」―
　しかし日本では神聖で最高に敬すべき存在としての天皇がいるが、クリスチャンはこれを生きた偶像でしかないと云っている。クリスチャンの中には天皇の写真の前で頭を下げる必要はないという人がいる*。このような人は本当の日本人ではない。従ってクリスチャンは国を敬う心に対して有害のものである。

*このような男は偽善者で無知蒙昧な人間である。自国では帽子も取らずに敢えて女王陛下の執事の部屋に入ることはないだろう。

[8] Composition:[What is the most awful thing?]　作文:[世に最も怖いものは何か？]

pectability of our country. ~~About~~ Nearly all ~~the~~ European races have the power of civilization without mercy, and are desirous to settle anywhere. If ~~the~~ Europeans ~~as come to interact~~ should settle in the interior of the country of Japan, they ~~will begin the~~ would establish a great commerce and commence ~~the rivality~~ "competition" is better with Japanese. We ~~will~~ would suffer a defeat. And ~~about all~~ the Europeans, would become very prosperous. They ~~will~~ would purchase many parts of the Yamato islands, and at last ~~there will~~ would become a dominion of some country of Europe — like India or ~~and~~ the many islands of the Pacific ocean. And by the doctrine of Sir ~~Cha~~ Charles Darwin, the Japanese race would ~~will~~ become European! by and by.*

†Not necessarily. You mean, of course, the doctrine of the "Survival of the fittest," which is no longer only a doctrine, but a positive truth. — I have, however, great faith in the force of the Japanese race.

100

*And a Consul is only an humble official of the Queen.

pectability of our country. ~~About~~ *Nearly*
all ~~the~~ European *races* have the power of
civilization without mercy, and ~~is~~ <are>
desirous to settle any-where. If ~~the~~
Europeans ~~can come to internal~~ *should settle in the interior of the* ∧ country
of Japan, they ~~will begin the~~ *would establish a* great
commerce and commence ~~the rivalry~~ *"competition" is better*
with Japanese. We ~~will~~ *would* suffer ~~a~~ defeat.
And ~~about all~~ the Europeans ∧ ~~is~~ *would become* very
prosperous. They ~~will~~ *would* purchase many
parts of ∧ *the* Yamato islands, and at
last, ~~i~~<t*hese*> ~~will~~ *would* become a dominion of
some country of Europe, ~~as~~ *-like* India *or* ~~and~~
the many islands ~~on~~ *of the* Pacific ocean.
And by the doctrine of Sir ~~Cho~~ Charles
Darwin, ∧ *the* Japanese race ∧ ~~will~~ *would* become
European by and by. *

*Not necessarily. You mean, of course, the
doctrine of the "Survival of the fittest," which
is no longer only a doctorine, but a
positive truth. —I have, however, great
faith in the force of the Japanese race.
$\overline{100}$
And a Consul is only an humble official of the Queen.

おそらく全てのヨーロッパの民族は情け容赦のない文明の力をもっており、何処にでも植民する野望をもっている。もしヨーロッパ人が日本の内部に植民して来たら、大きな経済力にまかせて日本と争うことになる。そして打ちのめされるのは我々の方だ。かくしてヨーロッパ人は皆栄え、彼らはこの大和の国の大部分を買収し最後には多くのインドや太平洋の島々のように日本を支配下に置くであろう。チャールズ・ダーウィン卿の原理に従って日本民族は少しずつヨーロッパのようになるであろう。*

*必ずしもそうではない。もちろん君は「適者生存」の学説を云っているのだろうが、これは最早単に学説といったものではなく、もっと積極的な真理というべきものなのだ。—それにしても、私は日本民族の力に大きな信頼を置いている。
$\overline{100}$
しかも執事は女王陛下に仕えるただの地位の低い役人にしかすぎないのだ。

編者注：最終行のハーンのコメント「*And a Consul is only an humble official of the Queen.*」は、前頁下のコメントからの続きである。

---

[8] Composition:[What is the most awful thing?]　作文：[世に最も怖いものは何か？]　39

Christianity will never be accepted in Japan, except by vulgar or weakminded people, — I trust. If the Buddhist schools would teach modern science, no Christian missionaries could proselytize the people. Out of 43,000,000 Japanese, the Christians themselves only claim to have about 60,000; and the probable truth is there are not more than 1 in 10 of these Christians in real belief.

Here are the texts, you referred to:—

— "A man shall leave his father and mother, and shall cleave unto his wife."
   Matthew. 19 chap. 5th verse.
  Also — Mark 10 " 7 "
  Also — Genesis 2 " 24 ".

These are the 3 texts of the Bible. In Europe, a wife does not wish to live with her husband's parents. Once married, the son abandons his parents, and helps them only in extreme cases. There is not in Europe, any of what is called filial piety in Japan, — except what the hearts of naturally good men make them do.

Christianity will never be accepted in Japan, except by vulgar or weakminded people, −I trust. If the Buddhist schools would teach modern science, no Christian missionaries could proselytize the people. Out of 43,000,000 Japanese, the Christians themselves only claim to have about 60,000; and the probable truth is there are not more than 1 in 10 of these Christians in real belief.

Here are the texts, you referred to:−
−"A man shall leave his father and mother, and shall cleave unto his wife."

Matthew.　19 chap. 5th verse.
Also − Mark　　10　〃　7　　〃
Also − Genesis　 2　〃　24　〃.

These are the 3 texts of the Bible. In Europe, a wife does not wish to live with her husband's parents. Once married, the son abandons his parents, and helps them only in extreme cases. There is not in Europe, any of what is called <u>filial piety</u> in Japan, − except what the hearts of naturally good men make them do.

キリスト教は粗野で少し精神の弱い人意外日本では受け入れられないだろう、−と私は信じる。もし仏教諸宗派が近代科学を教えていたとしたら、宣教師は誰一人として人々を改宗させることはできなかっただろう。4300万の日本人のうちクリスチャンは6万人程度といえるだけだ。そして恐らく当時こうしたクリスチャンのうち10人に1人も本当に信仰を持っていたとは思えない。ここに君が述べていた聖書からの引用がある。—
「人はその父と母を離れて、その妻と結ばれる。」
　　　　　　　　（マタイ、19章、5節）
さらに—（マルコ、10章、7節）
さらに—（創世記、2章、24節）
これは聖書から取った三つのテキストです。ヨーロッパでは妻は夫の両親と同居することを望まない。一度結婚したら息子は両親を捨て、余程のことがないと助けることはない。ヨーロッパには日本にあるような<u>慈悲深い哀れみ</u>の心がないのです。一例外的に生れつき良い心をもった人はそうしますが。

In India, the English have never been able to change the manners of the people, or to create a half-breed race. They are only rulers,— 1 Englishman to 100,000 Indians. In the Pacific islands, it is true they had their own way; but the inhabitants were only savages,— it was easy to oppress them. But Japan is a highly civilized country, and was civilized when all Europe was barbarous. To dominate Japan would be impossible,— except by a tremendous war. The very poverty of Japan is a source of strength. Japan has a population larger than that of any European country except Germany and Russia; and this immense Japanese population can live at one-tenth of the cost of life in Europe and can produce the same manufactures and industries at a far less cost. So that, in another fifty years, Japan ought to become one of the strongest countries in the world. Still, it would be best, that for another fifty years, foreigners should not be allowed to speculate in Japanese land or in Japanese labor. Russia, today, does not allow foreigners to do this.

In India, the English have never been able to change the manners of the people, or to create a half-breed race. They are only rulers, – 1 Englishman to 100,000 Indians. In the Pacific islands, it is true they had their own way; but the inhabitants were only savages, — it was easy to oppress them. But Japan is a highly civilized country, and was civilized when all Europe was barbarous. To dominate Japan would be impossible, — except by a tremendous war. The very poverty of Japan is a source of strength. Japan has a population larger than that of any European country except Germany and Russia; and this immense Japanese population can live at one= =tenth of the cost of life in Europe and can produce the same manufactures and industries at a far less cost. So that, in another fifty years, Japan ought to become one of the strongest countries in the world. Still, it would be best, that for another fifty years, foreigners should not be allowed to speculate in Japanese land or in Japanese labor. Russia, today, does not allow foreigners to do this.

インドにおいては、イギリス人は一度たりとも原地の人々のマナーを変えたり、混血の人種を作ることはできなかった。彼らはただの支配者で—10万人のインド人に対して1人のイギリス人という割合であった。太平洋の島々では彼ら流のやり方をすることは簡単にできた。しかし日本は今では高度に文明化された国であって、ヨーロッパが野蛮であった時でもすでに進んだ国であった。大きな戦争を起こすなら話は別だが、日本を支配することは不可能である。日本の貧しさというものはまさに力の源泉なのである。日本はドイツ、ロシアを除いてヨーロッパのどの国よりも人口が多い。この人口の多さによってヨーロッパの生活費の十分の一で生活し、はるかに安い費用でヨーロッパと同じだけの製品と生産量を生み出している。そこで50年もすれば日本はきっと世界でもっとも強い国の一つになるに違いない。さらにもっともうまくいった場合、さらにもう50年もすれば外国人たちは日本の国土や労働の世界に入りこめる見込みはなくなるであろう。ロシアでは今日外国人がこのようなことをすることはできない。

[9] Ghosts 幽霊

Composition.

M. Otani

Ghosts.

I have heard the word Ghost, but I do not know what a Ghost is. ~~Therefore~~ Nevertheless, I will write down a story about Ghost.

In ancient times, a knight was going to some town through silent villages. The evening came and the sun sunk behind western mountains. It was useless to go back, because, from that place, the nearest human dwelling was ~~ten~~ miles off. He anxiously scanned the country in the hope of finding a house. But a house was not in sight, and before him, a steep hill arope. He reached to the summit searching for a house, but it was in vain, when, far down the valley, he saw a small glittering light. He went toward it, and through the thick underbrush

Composition.

M. Ōtani

Ghosts.

I have hear̀ed the word Ghost, but
I do not know what ~~is~~ <a> Ghost <is>.
Nevertheless
~~Therefore~~, I will write down a
story about Ghost<s>.
In ancient time<s>, a knight
was going to some town through
silent villages.   The evening
       the   *behind*
came and ∧ sun sunk ~~to~~ western
mountains. It was useless to go
back because, from that place,
 nearest
the ∧ human dwellings was ten
miles off. He anxiously scanned
the country in the hope of finding
a house. But a house was not in
sight, and before him, a steep
         arose
hill ~~laid , lay down~~. He reached
              for a
to the summit searching ~~the~~ ∧ house,
but it was in vain, when, far
down the valley, ~~He~~ he saw a small
glittering light. He went toward
it, and through the thick underbrush

he reached to a house. He knocked, and the door was opened, and he asked for lodging for the night. His request was granted. That house was a old temple. He went to a room, and was soon asleep. By a sudden sound, he was awakened. It was dark night and he could hear the sound of rain falling. Just at his side, there was a sound like the gasping of a dying man. Then the damp and icy wind blew. A vivid blue flash of lightning illuminated that room. Suddenly there was a woman who had worn a white, long robe.⁽¹⁾ Her face was very pale, and her teeth was black, and her hair was so long that it reached the ground! It was a Ghost!

(1) Only a man's dress can be called a "coat", a woman's must be called a robe, or called by its Japanese name.

he reached ~~to~~ a house. He knocked, and the door was opened, and he asked for lodging for the night.

His request was granted. ~~It was permitted.~~ That house was a old temple. He went to a room, and was soon asleep. By a sudden sound, he was awakened. It was dark night and he could *her* hear the sound of rain falling. Just at his side, there was a ~~soud~~ sound like the gasping of a dying man. Then the damp and icy wind blew. A vivid, blue flash of lightning ~~was~~ illuminated ~~that in~~ that room. Suddenly there was a woman who had worn a white, long ~~coat~~ robe (1). Her face was very pale, and ~~his~~ her ~~teeths~~ teeth was black, and her hair was ~~very~~ long *so* ~~so~~ that it ~~was on~~ <reached> the ground.
It was a Ghost!

(1) *Only a man's dress can be called a "coat," – a woman's must be called a robe, or called by this Japanese name.*

民家の戸を叩くとドアが開いたので一晩泊めてもらうように頼みました。頼みは叶えられましたが、その家は古いお寺でした。彼は部屋に入るとすぐに眠り込んでしまいました。突然の音で彼は目が覚めました。その晩は暗くて雨の音がしていました。丁度何処からか死にそうな人のうめき声がすぐそばで聞こえてきました。それから湿った冷たい風が吹いてきました。ふいに鮮やかな青い稲妻が光って部屋が明るくなりました。突然、白い衣（ころも）(1)を着た女人がそこに立っていました。顔は真っ青で歯は黒く、髪の毛は長く、地面に横たわっていたのです。
それは幽霊だったのです！

(1) "*coat*" は男性についてのみ言えます。―女性の場合は必ず *robe* かこの語の日本名で言われます。

【10】The Birthday of His Majesty　天皇誕生日

Composition.
4. class M. Otani

†The Birthday of ~~Our~~ His Majesty.

The third of November is the birthday of Our Majesty. Japanese flags were hoisted above nearly every house. The lanterns were decorated with a Red Sun,— the national emblem of Japan. We assembled at our school at eight o'clock in the morning, and then performed the usual ceremony before the Emperor's photograph. We had some military exercise on at the hill which is called Shōgiyama and fired a salute. To celebrate the festival, the

(†) It would be better to say (1) "His Majesty the Emperor" or (2) "His Majesty Our Emperor."

Composition.
　　　　　4. class M. Otani

⁺ The Birthday of ~~Our~~ ///His///
　　Majesty.

The third of November is the birthday of Our Majesty.
　Japanese flags were hoisted
　above nearly every house.
The lanterns were decorated with
a Red Sun, – the national
emblem of Japan.
We assembled at ~~xxx~~ our school
at eight o'clock in the morning,
and then performed the
usual ceremony before the
Emperor's x photograph.
We had some military exercise
　　　on
~~at~~ ∧ the hill which is called
Shōgiyama and fired <a> salute.
To celebrate the festival, the ~~pageany~~

(+) *It would be better to say* ⁽¹⁾ "His Majesty the
　　Emperor" *or* ⁽²⁾ "His Majesty Our Emperor."

作文
　　　　4組　大谷　M.

⁺天皇誕生日

11月3日は天皇誕生日です。日本の国旗がほとんどどこの家にも掲げられました。提灯は赤い日の丸―日本の国旗で飾られました。学校では朝の8時に朝礼があり、ご真影の前で何時ものように儀式がとり行われました。床几山と言われる山では軍事訓練があり、敬礼を行いました。

(+) ⁽¹⁾ "His Majesty the Emperor." または ⁽²⁾ "His Majesty Our Emperor." と言った方が良い。

編者注：床几山（しょうぎやま）は堀尾吉晴公がその山頂より市中を眺め、この地に築城を定めた処といわれる。

pageants were displayed, and
all men drank wine and played
musical instruments.

(very good)

Pageant has the meaning of
"spectacle" — especially a brilliant
or magnificent spectacle. It
could not be used in this sense
with the word "performed."

pageants* ~~was~~ were ~~performed~~ *displayed* and all men dri<*a*>nk wine and played musical instruments.

この祭日を祝う出しもの*が出され、男性は全員お酒を飲み、楽器を演奏した。

(<u>very</u> good)

(<u>とても</u>良く出来ました)

<u>Pageant</u>* has the meaning of "spectacle" – especially a brilliant or magnificent spectacle. It could not be used in this sense with the word "performed."
———

<u>出しもの</u>*には「見せ場」の意味があります。―特に優れた素晴らしい見せ場の意味です。この語は "performed" と一緒に使われることはありません。
———

[10]　The Birthday of His Majesty　天皇誕生日

【11】 Composition: [Creator] 作文：[創造者]

Composition.

M. Ōtani

(1) A Book is made by a maker who is called the book-maker. Therefore the world must be made by a great maker also who is called the Creator.
Europeans are the civilized people.
(2) All Europeans believe in Christianity. Therefore, people who do not believe in Christianity can not be a civilized people.
Above sentences are not correct in the meaning totally, I think.

(1) This argument, (called by Christians Paley's Argument) is absurdly false. Because a book is made by a bookmaker, or a watch by a watchmaker, it does not follow at all that Suns and worlds are made by an intelligent designer. We only know of books and watches as human productions. Even the substance of a book or a watch we do not know the nature of. What we do know logically is that Matter is eternal, and also the Power which shapes it and changes it.
(2) Another false argument. At one time the

Composition.

M.Ôtani

(1) A Book is made by ~~the~~ a maker who is called the book-maker. Therefore the world must be made by a great maker also who is called the Creator.

The Europeans are ~~the~~ the most highly civilized people, (2) All Europeans believe <in> ~~the~~ Christianity. Therefore, ~~unless is the~~ people who do not believe ~~the~~ <in> Christianity can not be a civilized people.

The Above sentences are not correct in the meaning totally, I think.

(1) This argument, (called by Christians Paley's Argument), is absurdly <u>false</u>. Because a book is made by a bookmaker, or a watch by a watchmaker, it does not follow at all that Suns and worlds are made by an intelligent designer. We only know of books and watches as human productions. Even the substance of a book or a watch we do not know the nature of. What we <u>do</u> know logically is that Matter is eternal, and also the Power which shapes it and changes it.

(2) Another false argument.   At one time the

作文

大谷　M.

(1)本は本作りと呼ばれる作り手によって作られる。したがって、世界は創造主と呼ばれる偉大な作り手によって作られたにちがいない。ヨーロッパ人は、文明化された人々である。そして(2)すべてのヨーロッパ人は、キリスト教を信じている。ゆえに、キリスト教を信じない人々は、文明化されていないということになる。この文は、全く正しいことを伝えていないと私は思う。

(1) この考え方は、(クリスチャンたちにペイリーの議論と呼ばれているものだが) 全くの<u>偽り</u>である。
本は本作りによって、時計は時計職人によって作られるからといって、太陽やこの世界が知能の高い一人の設計者によって作られたということにはならない。われわれは本や時計については、それらは人間の作り出した産物であるということが分かっているだけである。われわれには本や時計という物の本質さえも分からないのです。論理的に<u>分かっている</u>ことといえば、物質は永遠であり、その物質を形づくり、変える力もまた永遠であるということである。

(2) もう一つの間違った議論。かって

Greeks and the Egyptians, both highly civilized people, believed in different gods. Later, the Romans and the Greeks, although highly civilized, accepted a foreign belief. Later still, these civilized peoples were conquered by races of a different faith. The religion of Mahomet was at one time that of the highest civilization. At another time, the religion of India was the religion of the highest civilization. It is very doubtful whether the civilization of a people has any connection whatever with their religion. — In Christian countries, moreover, the most learned men do not believe in Christianity; and the Christian religion is divided into countless sects, which detest each other. No European scientist of note — no philosopher of high rank, — no really great man is a Christian in belief —

Greeks and the Egyptians, both highly
civilized people, believed in different
gods. Later, the Romans and the
Greeks, although highly civilized, accepted
a foreign belief. Later still, these
civilized peoples were conquered by
races of a different faith. The
religion of Mahomet was at one time
that of the highest civilization. At
another time, the religion of India
was the religion of the highest
civilization. It is very doubtful
whether the civilization of a
people <u>has</u> any connection whatever
with their religion. – In
Christian countries, moreover, the most
learned men do not believe
in Christianity; and the Christian
religion is divided into countless
sects, which detest each other.
No European scientist of note —
no philosopher of high rank, —
no really great man is a
Christian in belief —

ギリシャ人やエジプト人は両者とも高度に文明化された人々でキリスト教とは異なった神々を信じていた。後にローマ人やギリシャ人は高度に進んだ文明をもってはいたが外国の信仰を受容した。しかしその後この高度な文明人は異なった信仰をもつ人々によって征服された。マホメット教はかつて最も高い文明を誇っていた宗教であった。またある時にはインドの宗教は最も高度に文明化された宗教であった。ある民族の文明がそれが何であれ宗教と何らかの関係が<u>ある</u>かどうかは疑わしい。―さらにキリスト教国ではもっとも教養ある人々はキリスト教を信じてはいない。そしてキリスト教も無数の宗派に分かれてお互いに憎み合っている。
ヨーロッパのすぐれた科学者も―
高名な哲学者も―
そして真に偉大な人物は
信仰において誰一人としてクリスチャンではない―

Composition.
                    4th U. Otani
    Boating on the lake of
         Shinji.

It is very pleasant to row and to sail X on the lake of Shinji. When the gusty tempests blow, and raging surges roll, ^a boat reels like a drunken man, and ^rocks like a cradled thing. When the weather is quiet and the surface of the lake is smooth, boats ~~do not~~ remain motionless ~~move~~ like ＆ anchored ships, and like ＆ sleepers. It is very pretty to look ^at ~~the~~ Mount Daisen which is covered with white and glittering snow, from the boat. And it is good scenery to ~~look~~ ^at the old castle called Kamedajō, which is a memorial of the feudal system of old Japan. In the boating on the lake,

Composition.

4ᵗʰ M.Ōtani

Boating on the lake of Shinji.

It is very pleasant to row and to sail ╳ on the lake of Shinji. When the gusty tempests blow, and raging surges roll, ∧ boat reels [*a*] like a drunken man, and ∧ like [*rocks*] a cradled thing. When the weather is quiet and the surface of the lake is smooth, boats ~~do not~~ [*remain*] ~~move~~ like ~~a~~ anchored ships, and [*motionless*] like ~~a~~ sleeper<s>. It is very pretty to look ~~the~~ Mount Daisen which [*at*] is covered with white and glittering snow, from the boat. And it is good scenery to look ∧ the old [*at*] castle called Kamedajō, which is a memorial of the feudal system of Old Japan. In the boating on the lake,

作文

4年　大谷　M.

宍道湖をボートで行くこと

宍道湖でボートを漕いだり帆走することはとても楽しい。突風や嵐が吹き、烈しい大波が打ち寄せる時は舟のリールが酔っ払いのようによろめき揺り篭のように大揺れする。天候が鎮まると、湖の表面は凪ぎ、ボートはまた元通り錨を降ろした舟、あるいは深く眠っている人のように静かになる。ボートから見える雪で白くかがやいて見える大山の景色は美しい。そして昔の日本の封建制度の象徴である亀田城と呼ばれる古城を見るのはいいものである。湖の上でボートを漕ぐと、

we exercise our bodies, and breathe the fresh air, and our eyes are amused by many beautiful landscapes round about the shore, and the boating on the lake is a health-giving ~~playing~~ amusement

28th, Feb.

good

we exercise our body~~y~~<*ies*>, and
breathe the fresh air, and
our eyes are amused by many
beautiful landscapes round
about the shore, and ~~the~~
boating on the lake is a
health-giving ~~playing~~ <*amusement*>

    28th, Feb.
     good

体の運動にもいいし、新鮮な空気を吸い込むことができる。そして目は岸辺の多くの美しい景色を愉しむことができる。湖面にボートを浮べることは健康に良い遊びなのである。

    2月28日
    よろしい

[12] Boating on the lake of Shinji 宍道湖をボートで行くこと

【13】The Tortoise 亀

Composition. —
4. M. Otani

The Tortoise.

A Japanese proverb says that "the life of the Japanese crane is measured to "one thousand years and the life of the tortoise is, ten thousands years." It is used generally as the emblem of long life in any celebration. Its back is ~~the~~ ^very^ hard and is regularly divided by ~~the cut~~ ^seams, or lines^ into many hexagonal shapes. It is said that the old tortoise has ^a^ very long and beautiful tail which consists of many thousand hairs. Its head and feet can be hidden under its ~~back~~ ^shell^.(¹) From the shell of a tortoise which lives in the ocean, we can make ~~the~~ ^various^ ornaments, ~~like the~~ ^such as^ ornamental hair-pins. It is said that

(¹). Better to say: "It can hide its head and feet under (or inside of) " &c.

Composition.

4. M.Ōtani

The Tortoise.

A *the*
˄Japanese proverb says that "the life of ˄Japanese crane is measured to one thousand years and the life of the tortoise is ten thousands years." It is used generally as the emblem of long life in any celebration. Its *very* back is ~~the~~ ˄hard and is regular- *seams, or lines* ly divided by ~~the cut~~ <*in* >to many hexagonal shapes. It is said *a* that the old tortoise has ˄very long and beautiful tail which consists of many thousand hairs. Its head and feet can be hidden *shell* under its ~~back~~.(1) From the shell of a tortoise which lives in the ocean, we can make *various* *such as* ~~the~~ ˄ornaments, ~~like the~~ ornamental hair-pins. It is said that

(1) *Better to say*: "It can hide its head and feet) under(_____ " &c.
(or "inside of")

作文

4．大谷　M.

亀

日本には「鶴は千年亀は万年」という諺がある。これはおめでたい席で一般的に長寿の象徴として用いられる。甲羅はとても硬くきれいに六角形の区切れあるいは境界線で分けられている。年寄りの亀は数千本の毛でできたとても長くて美しい尾をもっているとされている。頭と足は甲羅の下に隠している。(1)海亀の甲羅からはヘアピンのような種々の飾りものを作ることができる。

(1) "It can hide its head and feet)under(_____ " &c. と言った方がよい。
(or "inside of")

The snapping-turtle likes very much to drink wine.⁽¹⁾ So among old pictures, there is one in which the tortoise and wine cups drawn. In Japan, there are many anecdotes about the tortoise.

or: "is very fond of drinking wine."

~~Th~~ the snapping-turtle ~~is~~<*likes*> very ~~fond~~ *much*
to drink ~~the~~ wine.⁽¹⁾ So, ∧ ~~in the~~ *among*
old pictures, there ~~x~~ is one ∧ *in* which
~~is drawn~~ the tortoise and wine
cup ~~is~~<*are*> drawn. In Japan, there are
many anecdotes about the tortoise.

      or: "*is very fond <u>of</u> drinking
      wine.*"

噛み付き亀は酒を飲むのが好きだ。⁽¹⁾それで昔の絵には亀と盃が描かれている。日本では亀についての逸話が多い。

      または："*is very fond <u>of</u> drinking wine.*"とする。

[13] The Tortoise 亀 63

【14】Lake Shinji　宍道湖

Composition.

4th M. Ōtani

~~The~~ Lake Shinji.

~~The~~ Lake Shinji is the greatest lake in ~~the western~~ countries ~~from~~ ^{west of} Kiyōto, and lies in the north part of Idzumo. There are many beautiful landscapes round about the shores of this lake. When the weather is fine the surface of the lake is quiet and calm like as looking-glass, and when the winds blow the heaving and raging surges roll and foam⁽¹⁾ ~~like as many soaring sea-gulls~~. In the summer evening, it is very pleasant to row on the lake to enjoy the cool breeze which springs up at sunset. In the autumn, when the golden moon rises the eastern mountains and ^{their} ~~its~~ shade^{ws are} reflected ^{upon} ~~to~~ the surface of the lake, ~~it~~ ^{The moonshine seems to make} makes ~~the~~ silver path ^{over a} ~~upon the~~ pavement of saphire. ~~It is best~~ ^{The first} scenery ^{is that of looking toward} ~~to look~~ the mount Daisen and ^{the view of the} old castle from

⁽¹⁾ The English is correct; but the thought is wrong. Seagulls do not roar or foam.

Composition.

               4th M.Ōtani

~~The~~ Lake Shinji.

~~The~~ Lake Shinji is the greatest lake in ~~the western~~ countries ~~from~~ ^*west of*^ Kiyoto, and lies in the north part of Idzumo. There are many beautiful landscapes round about the shores of this lake. When the weather is fine the surface of the lake is quiet and calm like as looking-glass, and when the winds blow the heaving and raging surges roll and foam (1)~~like as many soaring see-gulls~~. In the summer evening, it is very pleasant to row on the lake to enjoy the cool breeze which springs up at sunset. In the autumn, when the golden moon rises the east<ern> mountain<s> and ~~its~~ <their> shade<ows are> reflects<ed> ^upon^ ~~to~~ the surface of the lake. ~~it~~ ^*The moonshine*^ makes ~~the~~ ^*seems to make a*^ silver path ~~upon the~~ ^*over a*^ pavement of sa<p>phire. ~~It is best~~ ^*The finest*^ scenery ~~to look the~~ ^*is that looking toward*^ mount Daisen and ^*the view of the*^ old castle from

  (1) The English is correct; but the thought is wrong. Seagulls do not roar or foam.

作文

            4年　大谷 M.

宍道湖

宍道湖は京都から西方で一番大きな湖であって出雲の北部に位置している。湖畔には美しい景色が多い。天候が良いと湖面は鏡のように静かで穏やかである。風が吹くと大揺れの波が打ち寄せて泡吹いてくる(1)。夏の夜に湖でボートを漕いで夕日に湧き立つ涼風を楽しむことはとても楽しいことだ。満月が上がる秋には東の山々とその影が湖面に銀色に映えてサファイアのような道が出来る。一番すばらしい光景は

(1) 英語は正しいが思考は間違っている。鷗はうなったり泡吹いたりしない。

編者注：ハーンは大谷学生の書いた英作文10行目のsoarをroarと読み間違えたようだ。

the small island named Yomega-shima which is situated at the ~~east and~~ south east ~~south~~ part of the Lake Shinji.

very good indeed.

the small island named Yomega-shima which is situated at the ~~east and south~~ <u>south east</u> part of the Lake Shinji.

very good indeed.

宍道湖の南東に位置する嫁ヶ島と呼ばれる小さい島から見える大山と古城の景色である。

とてもよく出来ている

【15】About Kasuga at Matsue　松江の春日について

Composition.

5th M. Otani

About Kasuga at Matsue.

On a hill which is situated at the north west part of Matsue, there is a shrine called Kasuga. From that hill we can see nearly all the streets of Matsue. It is a very quiet and shady place, and good for walking and breathing the fresh air. There are many large cherry-trees and many exuberant tsutsuji shrubs. So we can take the pleasure of seeing them in their flowering seasons. As the servants guards of the god of Kasuga, there are the statues of a couple of deer.

The following sentences do not relate only to Kasuga at Matsue, but to every Shinto shrines. First we can see the statues of a couple of lions (kara-shishi). I think they mean the protectors of god.* The lion is the king of

*The karashishi are of Buddhist origin, although adopted by Shinto, since the time of Ryōbu-Shintō

Composition.

    5th M. Otani

About Kasuga at Matsue.

On a hill which is situated at the north west part of Matsue, there is a shrine called Kasuga. From that hill we can see nearly all ^the streets of Matsue. It is ^a very quiet and shady <good> place, and ~~able~~ for walking and breathing the fresh air. There are many large cherry-trees and many exuberant tsutsuji shrubs. So we can take the pleasure of seeing them in their flowering seasons. As *servants* the ~~guards~~ of the god of Kasuga, there are the statues of a couple of *deer* ~~deers~~.

 The following sentences do not *relate* ~~concern~~ only to ~~ka~~ Kasuga at Matsue, but to every Shinto shrines. First we can see the statues of a couple of lions (kara-shishi). I think they mean the protectors of god.* The lion is the king of

*The karashishi are of Buddhist origin, although adopted by Shintō, since the time of Ryōbu-Shintō.

作文

    5年　大谷　M.

松江の春日について

松江の北西に位置する小高い山の上に春日と呼ばれる神社がある。ここからはほぼ松江の街のすべてが見える。ここは静かで木蔭が多く、散歩と新鮮な空気を吸うのにもってこいのところだ。ここには桜の木が多く躑躅が繁茂している。そこで花の咲くころにこれらの花を見ることは楽しいことである。春日神社の神に仕えるのは二匹の鹿の像である。

　次の文は松江の春日に関係するだけでなく、全ての神道の神社に関係する。まず、ここでは一対の獅子の像（唐獅子）が見られる。私にはこれは神*の護衛のように思われる。獅子は百獣の王で

*唐獅子は両部神道の時代から神道に取り入れられたが、その源は仏教に由来する。

animals and is very strong and very terrible, but it is not an proper animal of Japan, and has no connection with the gods of Japan. It will be true that it came from Buddhist. Next, there is a Torii (Tori = bird, i = inhabitation). I think, in Japan there are two kinds of Torii, as following shapes: —

(1)   (2)

(1) thing is ordinary and (2) thing is rare. Some man says, (2) one is the primary thing which was used in Old Japan, and (1) is its developed thing. The other says that, (2) thing is the proper Torii of Japan and (1) came from Buddhist. I can not understand why it is erected before the gate of every temples. Some man says it is only the perch of the sacred

animals and is very strong and very
terrible, but it is not <an> ~~proper~~ animal
of ~~of~~ Japan, and ~~have~~ <has> no connection ~~to~~ <with>
       is certain
the gods of Japan. It ~~will be true~~
that it came from Buddhist<*m*>.
Next, there is a <u>Torii</u> (Tori=bird, i=
inhabitation). I think, in Japan
there are two kinds of <u>Torii</u>, as following shapes:——

  (1)   (2)

(1) thing is ordinary and (2) thing is
rare. Some man says, (2) one is the
primary thing which was used in Old
Japan, and (1) is its developed thing.
~~The~~ <*An*>other says that, (2) thing is the
proper <u>Torii</u> of Japan and (1) came
from Buddhist.   I can not
understand why it is erected before
the gate of every temple~~s~~. Some man
says it is only the perch of the sacred

とても強く、とても恐ろしい。しかしそれは日本古来の動物ではなく、日本の神々とは何の関係もない。それは紛れもなく仏教から来たものである。

　次に鳥居（Tori＝鳥、i＝居）がある。日本には次のような二種類の形の鳥居がある。

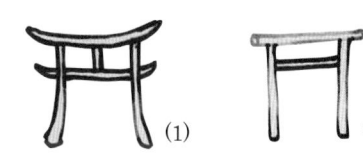

  (1)   (2)

(1)は通常のもので(2)は珍しい。ある人によると(2)は古代の日本で用いられていた原始的なものであり、(1)はそれが発達したものである。別の人によれば、(2)が本来の日本の鳥居で(1)は仏教から来たものであるという。何故すべての神社の前に鳥居が立てられているか私にはわからない。ある人によればそれは

birds of the god. The other says, it is a piece of the symbols which was built at four sides of the sepulchers of gods.* The Torii at Kasuga is made of stone. Next, in the gate there are two statues of armed men, who have quivers of arrows at their backs and the bows in their hands. There are called dzuijin (dzui = placed under, jin = god). One of them keeps its mouth unclosed and the other keeps it closed. One man says that they are not the shapes of two men, but the young shape and old shape of Tachikara-ono-mikoto. Some Buddhist priest said to me that it came from Buddhists (He was perhaps right!) The statue that keeps its mouth unclosed is the shape which is pronouncing the sound $\bar{a}$, and the statue that keeps it closed is the shape which is pronouncing the sound $\underline{n}$. In the Japanese alphabet, $\bar{a}$ is the

* — Mr. Satow gives one explanation of the torii as a perch for birds. Mr. Aston gives another, and I think it better, — from "toru" to pass through, and "iru", to dwell. But nobody is sure what the torii's origin is.

birds of ^*the* god. The other says, it is a
piece of the symbols which was built
at ^*the* four side<s> of the sepulchers of gods.*
<The> Torii at Kasuga is made of stone.
Next, in the gate there are two statues of
armed ma<e>n, who have ~~the~~ ^*quivers of* arrows at
the<ir> back<s> and ~~the~~ bow<s> in the<ir> hand<s>.
~~It is~~ ^*These are* called dzuijin (dzui=placed
under, jin=god).   One of them keep<s>
its mouth unclosed and the other
keep<s> ^*it* closed.   One man says that,
they are not the shapes of two men, but
the young shape and old shape of
Tachikara ~~no~~ onomikoto.   Some
Buddhist priest said to me that it
came from Buddist<m>. | *He was perfectly right!* | The statue
that keeps its mouth unclosed is the
shape which is pronouncing the
sound ă, and the statue ~~whi~~
that keeps <it> closed is the shape which
is pronouncing the sound n.
In <the> Japanese alphabet, ă is the

* — Mr. Satow gives one explanation of the Torii as a perch for birds. Mr. Aston gives another, and I think a better, − from "torù" to pass through − and "iru", to dwell. But nobody is sure what the Torii's origin is.

ただ神聖な神の鳥が留まるところに過ぎないという。他の人は神々の聖墓の４側面に置かれる象徴なのだという。春日の鳥居は石で出来ている。

次に、入り口の所では戦の格好をした二体の立像がある。背中には矢筒に入った矢を背負い、手には弓をもっている。これらの像は随神（随＝下位にある、神＝神）と呼ばれている。そのうち一方は口を開き、他方は閉じている。ある人によればこれは二人の兵士の像ではなく、タヂカラオノミコトの若い時と老いた時の形とのこと。ある僧侶によればこれは仏教から来たとのこと。（彼の言い分は全く正しい！）口を開いている像は「ア（ă）」の音を発している像である。口を閉じている像は「ン（n）」の音を表している像である。日本語の五十音では「ア（ă）」は

＊サトー氏は鳥居の説明として鳥の止まり木としている。アストン氏は他の説明をしている。私はこちらの説明がいいと思うのだが、それは「通る」(pass through) と「居る」(dwell) から来ているとする説である。しかし誰も「鳥居」の本当の起源を知る者はいない。

編者注：ハーン解説中の"torù"は"tòru"(to pass through) の間違いであろう。

[15] About Kasuga at Matsue 松江の春日について   73

beginning and n is the end. So, the shapes of Dzuijin means that, all things that have the beginning must have the end. (The All human beings must die.) In a little shrine near the Torii of Kasuga, there are three statues of monkeys. One of them conceals his eyes. The Second of them conceals his mouth mouth. The Third of them conceals his ears. I do not know the origin of them.

Please pardon me of having composed long one.

("mouth open" is better than "mouth unclosed".)

— 100 —

Among the Greeks also the first and last letters of the alphabet had the same sacred meaning. Thus the God of the Gospels says: "I am the Alpha (A) and the Omega (Ω)." — i.e. the Beginning and the End. And we say in English still, — "From Alpha to Omega."

beginning and n is the end.   So, the shapes of Dzuijin means that, all things that have the beginning must have ∧ end. (T̶h̶e̶ <*All*> human being<*s*> must die.)   In a little shrine near <*the*> Torii of Kasuga, there are three statues of monkeys. One of them conceals his eyes. <*The*> Second of them conceals his m̶o̶u̶t̶h̶s̶ mouth. <*The*> Third of them conceals his ears.   I do not know the origin of them.

Please pardon me of having composed long one.

("mouth open" is better than "mouth unclosed")

—— 100 ——

Among the Greeks also the first and last letters of the alphabet had the same sacred meaning. Thus the God of the Gospels says: "I am the Alpha (A) and the Omega(Ω)." – i.e. the Beginning and the End. And we say in English still, – "from Alpha to Omega."

始まりで「ン」は終りである。そこで、随神の形は始まりのあるものは全て終りがあるということを意味している。人間は必ず死ぬ。春日神社の鳥居の近くの小さな神社には猿の像が三つある。一匹目は目を閉じ、二匹目は口を閉じ、三匹目は耳を閉じている。私はその謂れは知らない。

長い作文を書いてしまったことをお許し下さい。

("mouth open"の方が"mouth unclosed"よりも良い。)

——100——

ギリシャ語の中でアルファベットの最初と最後の文字は神聖な意味をもっている。かくして福音書の神は「私はアルファ（A）でありオメガ（Ω）である」つまり始まりであり終りである、と言っている。そして英語では今も「アルファからオメガまで」と言う。

[15]   About Kasuga at Matsue   松江の春日について   75

【16】The Japanese Monkey　日本猿

Composition.

10th day.

The Japanese Monkey.

The monkey which lives in Japan belongs to the Innus. speciosus variety of Quadrumana. He lives on high mountains. He is a very active and cunning animal and very ~~like~~ fond of play. The face of this monkey is very red and his tail is not ~~very~~ long. Once I went to a temple and found the carvings of three different monkeys. ~~One of which~~ One monkey covers his eyes with both ~~his~~ ~~both~~ hands, and another ~~one~~ ~~other~~ covers his ears, and the third ~~last thing~~ covers his mouth. But we do not know what ~~do~~ they mean.

— The Apes of Koshin. They have a very interesting meaning, worth finding out.

4th. year class.

M. Ōtani

Composition.
          10th day.
  The Japanese Monkey.

T~~he~~y monkey which lives in
                    the
Japan belongs to ∧ Innus speciosus
     variety
∧ of Quadrumana. He lives i<*o*>n
                  a
high mountains. He is ∧ very active
and cunning animal and very
fond of
~~like to~~ play. The face of
this monkey is very red and
              very
his tail is not ~~so~~ long. Once
I went to a temple and found
the carvings of three different
monkeys. ~~One of which~~
One monkey covers his eyes
       both   *another*
with ∧ his ~~both~~ hands, and ~~one
of others~~ covers his ears, and
           third
the ~~last thing~~ covers his mouth.
But we do not know what ~~do~~
they mean.

   −The Apes of Koshin. They have a
    very interesting meaning, worth
    finding out.
                4th. year class.
                M. Ōtani

作文
                        10日
         日本猿

　日本猿は学名 四足哺乳動物の Innus Speciosus に属し、高い山中に住んでいる。よく動きずる賢い動物で遊びが好きである。顔はとても赤く尾はそれ程長くない。お寺に行ったとき、三種類の猿の彫り物がありました。一つ目の猿は目を両手で蓋っている。別の猿は耳を蓋い、三番目の猿は口を蓋っている。しかしその意味するところはわかりません。

　―庚申の猿である。その意味は調べてみるだけの値打ちがありますよ。

                4年級
                大谷　M.

[16]　The Japanese Monkey　日本猿　　77

Composition.

M. Otani's
The Fashions of Old Japan.
Part I — The House.

In the age of the gods, the people of Japan ~~almost~~ generally ~~inhabited~~ dwelt (or lived) in ~~the~~ caves. The people ~~that~~ who ~~inhabited~~ lived in the houses ~~which is made~~ built of wood, w~~er~~e very few ~~rare~~. There were two kinds of cave — stone caves and earth caves. It is said that Amaterashi ōka[1] being angry about the violence of ~~her brother~~ Susanoonomikoto, hid ~~to~~ herself in a stone cave which is called Amano-iwaya, and the world became dark. And stone caves w~~as~~ere the ~~house~~ dwelling that people of high rank lived in, and the people of humble rank inhabited ~~in~~ earth caves. At the mouth of every cave, a large stone or tree ~~wood~~ was placed as a "door". High people w~~as~~ere accustomed to spread out ~~the~~ coarse mats and sleep on them, and to cover the body with a cotton blanket. But

---

[1] Amaterasu-omi-Kami, being a goddess, the pronoun must be feminine.

Composition.

M. Ōtani

The fashions of Old Japan.
Part I – The House.

In the age of <*the*> gods, the people of Japan ~~almost~~ *generally* ~~inhabited~~ *dwelt (or lived)* in ~~the~~ caves. The people ~~that inhabited~~ *who lived* in ~~the~~ house<*s*> ~~which is~~ *built* ~~made~~ of wood, was<*ere*> very ~~rare~~ *few*. There were two kinds of cave – stone caves and earth caves. It is said that Amaterashiōka(1) being angry about the violence of his<*er*> brother Susanoonomikoto, hid ~~to~~ *herself in a* stone cave which is called Amano-iwaya, and the world became dark. And stone cave<*s*> was<*ere*> the ~~house~~ *dwellings* that *people of* high rank lived in, and *the people of* humble rank inhabited ~~in~~ earth caves. ~~In~~<*At*> the mouth of every cave, *a* large stone or ~~wood~~ *tree* was placed as *a* door. High people was<*ere*> accustomed to spread out ~~the~~ coarse mats and sleep on ~~it~~ <*them*>, and to cover the body with *a* cotton blanket. But

(1) *Amaterasu-omi-kami, being a goddess, the pronoun must be feminine.*

作文

大谷　M.

古代日本の様式
そのI―住居

神世の時代、日本人は一般的に洞窟に住んでいた。木の家に住んでいた人は稀であった。洞窟には二種類あって－石の洞窟と土の洞窟であった。アマテラスオオミカミ (1) がスサノオノミコトの暴力に怒って天の岩屋と言われる石の洞穴に身を隠したので世界が真っ暗になった。そして石の洞窟は地位の高い人々が住む住まいであり、地位の低い人々は土の洞窟に住んでいた。洞窟の入口には大きな石または木が扉として置かれていた。地位の高い人々は目の粗い茣蓙を広げその上に寝て体は木綿の布で被っていた。しかし

(1) 天照大神は女神なので代名詞は女性形でなければいけません。

> I do not understand this word

humble people spread out the reeds and *brundo* and slept on stem, and did not use the blankets, but only straw clothing. In the age of Jinmu who was the founder and first emperor of Japan, there was savage natives who were called Tsuchigumo⁽¹⁾ Tsuchi (earth) gomori (inhabit). The palace of Jinmu, which was situated in Kashiwabara of Yamato, was built with wood, and the column was called Amenomihashira, and every pillar was bound with vines. But earth caves was used as late as the 9th century. In the age of Ojintennō, the intercourse with Sankan having begun, the construction of houses changed.

⁽¹⁾ The generally-accepted meaning of Tsuchigumo is "Earth-spider"; and in old Japanese books these cave dwellers are pictured as enormous spiders. — Still, some say the word is a corruption of tsuchi-gomori, which would mean "Earth-hiders." Such is the opinion of the translator of the Ko-ji-ki.

I do not understand this word.

humble people spread out ~~the~~ reeds and Arundo and slept on ~~it~~ <them> and did not use ~~the~~ blankets but only straw clothing. In the age of Jinmu who was the founder and first emperor of Japan, there was<ere> savage natives ~~which is~~ who were called Tsuchigumo[1] ~~which means~~ from Tsuchi (earth) gomori (inhabit). The palas<c>e of Jinmu, which was situated in Kashiwabara of Yamato was built with wood, and the column was called Amenomihashira, and every pillar was ~~bind~~ <bound> with vines. But earth caves was<ere> used as late as the 9th century. In the age of Ojintennō, ~~the~~ intercourse with ~~of~~ Sankan having begun, the ~~structure~~ construction of houses ~~had~~ changed.

[1] The ~~real~~ generally = accepted meaning of Tsuchi gumo is "Earth-spider"; and in old Japanese books these cave dwellers are pictured as enormous spiders. — Still, some say the word is a corruption of ~~Tsucho~~ tsuchi-gomori, which would mean "Earth-hiders." Such is the opinion of the translator of the Ko-ji-ki.

この語は何かわかりません

卑しい身分の人たちはい草と Arundo を広げそしてその上に寝て、毛布ではなく藁でできた服を着ていた。日本の基礎をつくり最初の天皇となった神武の時代にはツチ（土）ゴモリ（住む）に由来するツチグモ[1]と呼ばれる原始の人々がいた。神武の宮殿は大和の柏原にあって木で出来ており、柱は天の御柱と呼ばれ、柱はすべて蔓で絡ませていた。そして土の洞窟は9世紀頃まで使われていた。応神天皇の時代に三韓との交渉が始まって家の造りが変ったのである。

[1] 一般的に容認された「土蜘蛛」の意味は「土―蜘蛛」であり、古い日本の文献では、これら洞窟居住者は巨大な蜘蛛として描かれている。—さらにこの語彙は「土に隠れるもの」を意味する「土篭り」の訛ったものという人もいる。これは『古事記』の訳者の考え方である。

編者注：Arundo は、い草のような背の高い草の一種（arundo donax）。

Reeds are generally larger and harder than what were used, both in England and Japan in old days, to sleep upon. The smaller and softer marsh-plants are called rushes. In old English castles the stone floors were always covered with rushes.

Reeds are generally larger and harder than what were used, both in England and Japan in old days, to sleep upon. The smaller and softer marsh-plants are called <u>rushes</u>. In old English castles the stone floors were always covered with rushes.

葦は通常かつて古代のイングランドや日本で寝るのに使われていたものよりも大きくて硬い。もっと小さくて柔らかいもの（植物）は<u>い草</u>と呼ばれる。古代のイングランドのお城では石の床にはいつもい草が敷かれていた。

[18] The Fashions of Old Japan Part II—The Clothing　古代日本の様式　そのⅡ—衣服

Composition
　　　4th　　M. Otani

The fashions of Old Japan.
　　Part II — The Clothing.

In Old Japan, there was only a kind of clothing, which was called chihaya. The Nihonki (?), the famous history of Old Japan, says that, Izanami-no-mikoto threw down his girdle and it became Nagachi-iwa-no-kami, and threw down his coat and it became Wadzurai-no-kami, and threw down his loose trowsers(1) and they became Akikui-no-kami. And it is said that, Amaterashi-ōkami knotted the skirt of her garment, and made loose trow-sers (hakama). Therefore it can be certainly supposed that, the clothing was used in Old Japan. The clothing was buttoned on the left side. Many precious stones were hung around the neck. The girdle was tied with Tamaki (Kushiro) which means Te (hand)

(1) "Trowsers" — always plural, unless you say, a "pair of trowsers."

[margin notes: There are several books which nearly the same name in Japan. I can't get you whether it be the Nihongi, or "Chronicles of the Japan" is very different from Kojiki. Translator spelt NIHONGI]

There are several books with nearly the same name in English letters. I think you mean the very old "Nihongi," – or "Chronicles." The text is very different from the Kojiki. Translators spell NIHONGI.

Composition

4th   M. Ōtani

The fashions of Old Japan.

Part II – The Clothing.

In ~~the~~ o<O>ldJapan, there was only a kind of clothing, which ~~is~~ *was* called ~~Ch~~ chihaya. <The>*Nihonki (g?), the famous history of Old Japan, says that, Izanami-no-mikoto threw ^*down* his girdle and it became Nagachi-iwa-no-kami, and threw ^*down* his coat and it became Wadzurai-no-kami, and threw ^*down* his loose trowsers(1) and ^*they* became Akikui-no-kami. And it is said that, Amaterashi-ōkami knotted the skirt of ^*her* garment, and ^*so* made ~~the~~ loose trowsers (hakama). Therefore it can *certainly* be supposed that ~~there was in certain the~~ clothing ^*was used* in Old Japan. The clothing was buttoned on the left side. Many precious stones were hung~~ed~~ around the neck. The girdle was tied with Tamaki (Kushiro) which means Te (hand)

(1) "Trowsers" – always plural, unless you say, a "pair of trowsers."

作文

4年　大谷　M.

古代日本の様式

そのⅡ－衣服

昔の日本では千早と呼ばれる一種類の衣服しかありませんでした。有名な古代の日本史である日本記によれば、イザナミノミコトが腰のベルトを投げ落とすとそれがナガチイワノカミとなりました。上衣（コート）を投げ落とすとワズライノカミとなり、緩んだズボンを投げ落とすとそれはアキクイノカミとなりました。そしてアマテラシ・オオカミが自らの衣服のスカートを編んで緩やかなズボン（ハカマ）を作ったのです。したがって衣服が古代の日本で使われていたことは確かです。ボタン止めは左側でした。首の周りには貴重な宝石をつけていました。腰帯は手を意味する鐶（釧）に結びつけられていました。

(1) "Trowsers"は a "pair of trowsers" と言わない場合を除いては常に複数形です。

英語でほぼ同じような名前の本がいくつかある。君はおそらくとても古い『日本記』か『年代記』のことを言っているのではないだろうか。本文は『古事記』とはかなり違っている。訳者はNIHONGIと綴っている。

[19] To Mr. Lafcadio Hearn　ラフカディオ・ハーン先生へ

Composition.
　　　　In Matsue Chūgakkō,
　　　　　June. 20th, XXIV.

To Mr. Lafcadio Hearn.

Dear sir,

　　Allow me to present you with a letter. As soon as I ~~passed~~ (I have) passed our fourth class in the annual examination of this year, I will take a journey ~~among~~ (through) Idzumonokuni. The object of this journey is to collect the plants and insects for ~~the~~ specimens of natural history. But I desire to go to bathe in the sea ~~of~~ (at) Kidzuki, and to visit the old Buddhist temples and Shinto shrines in Idzumonokuni. I heard that you are intending ~~to take a~~ (have) travel~~ling~~ in Idzumonokuni to search for materials for anthropology. If it ~~will~~ be true, I hope to travel with you.

Composition.

In Matsue Chûgakkô.
June 20th, XXIV.

作文

松江中学校にて
6月20日、24.

To Mr. Lafcadio Hearn.
Dear sir,
   Allow me to present you with a letter. As soon as I ^*have* passed our fourth class in the annual examination of this year, I will take a journey ~~among~~ *through* Idzumo no kuni. The object of this journey is to collect the plants and insects for ~~the~~ specimens of natural history. But I desire to go to bath<e> in the sea ~~of~~ <at> Kidzuki, and to visit the old Buddhist temples and Shintô shrines in Idzu-monokuni. I ^*have* heard that you are intending to ~~take a~~ traveling in *(or to take a trip through)* Idzumonokuni to search for materials for anthropology. If it ~~will~~ be true, I hope to travel~~l~~ with you.

ラフカディオ・ハーン先生へ
親愛なる先生、
　手紙をお送りすることをお許し下さい。今年の学年末の4年生の試験を通過できれば出雲の国を旅するつもりです。この旅の目的は理科の標本作りのための植物や昆虫を採集することです。しかし杵築の海で泳ぎ、出雲の国の古い仏閣や神社を訪ねたいとも思っています。私は先生が人類学の資料を探すために出雲の国の旅をなさりたいと伺っております。もしそれが本当なら私は先生と一緒に旅をしたいと思っております。

yours respectfully,
Masanobu. Otani

R. S. V. P.

             yours respectfully,   敬具
          Masanobu, Ōtani   大谷　正信

R.S.V.P.   R.S.V.P.

        99   99

[20] Fencing 剣道

Composition.
4th class
M. Ōtani

~~The~~ Fencing.

~~The~~ Fencing is the art ~~of~~ that teaches ^how to use the sword well. [I] It ~~was~~ used ~~among the~~ practised by soldiers for war in ~~the~~ old Japan; but at the present time it is ~~used among~~ practised by ~~the~~ young men as a healthful ~~playing~~ exercise. In ancient times there was the knight who was called musha-shigiyō. ~~The knight of ancient time~~ The habit of the knight of ancient time was that he traveled in all ~~countrys~~ parts of Japan and fenced in the houses of celebrated fencers, about which ~~Japan~~ custom ~~contain~~ the many curious and interesting stories are told in Japan. In the gymnastic contest of next Saturday we will take

Composition.

4th class

M. Ōtani

~~The~~ f<*F*>encing.

~~The~~ f<*F*>encing is the art ~~of~~ that
how
teaches ∧ to use the sword well. [I]It
 practised by
was ~~used among the~~ soldiers for
war in ~~Ol~~ old Japan, but at the
 practised by
present time it is ~~used among~~
~~the~~ young men as a healthful
 exercise
~~playing~~ ∧. In ancient times
there was the knight who was
called musha-shigiyō. ~~The~~
~~knight of ancient times~~ The
habit of the knight of ancient
time was that he traveled in
 parts
all ~~countrys~~ of Japan and
fenced in the houses of
celebrated fencers, about which
custom
~~Japan contain the~~ many
curious and interesting story<*ies*>.
are told in Japan.
In the gymnastic contest of
next Saturday we will ~~take~~

作文

4組

大谷 M.

剣道

剣道は剣を巧みに使う方法を教える技術である。それは昔日本では武士たちが実戦の場で使っていたものである。しかし現在では若者が健康的な運動として活用している。昔、武者修行をする侍がいた。古代の侍の習慣として日本中を旅し、名の通った剣士のいる道場で手合わせをしていた。この習慣については多くの不思議な興味深い話が伝えられている。来週土曜日の運動会では

have a fencing ~~match~~ match of the following kind:—
All the scholars of the school will be ~~detached~~ divided into two parts; and the eyes of all will be covered with ~~a~~ something so that they can scarcely see the sunlight, and they will strike the symbol which is placed at the head of every scholar. I think, this playing is very good for us, because it is the best exercise to cultivate a courageous character.

```
         have           = match of the following kind: −
   ∧a fencing which manner
                    thing
seems to be such ∧ that
          the       the
<A>all ∧ scholars of ∧ school <will be>
  divided
detached <in>to two parts; and <the>
<eyes of> all men's eyes will be covered
       something
with anythings so that they
can scarcely see the Sunlight,
    they will try to
and ∧ strike the symbol which
is placed at the head of every
scholars.    I think, this
playing is very good for us,
                    exercise
because it is the best playing
    cultivate a
to raise the courageous
character.
```

次のような種類の剣道の試合をすることになっている。

　学生は全員二つのパートに分けられ、全員目隠しをされるので陽光はほとんど見えない。学生たちは頭につけた目印を撃とうと奮闘する。私は、この競技は私たちにとって大変良いものと思う。それは、勇気を養うのに最も適したものであるからである。

Composition. 4th class.
                M. Ōtani

About the Gymnastic Contest of Last
        Saturday.

I could not play myself at the gymnastic=contest of last saturday, because I have hurt my heart a little. Therefore I will write down about the playings which I saw at it.

The weather was very fine for October, and it was a very good day for the contest. I went to my school at eight oclock at morning, but all my friends had started for Ninomal which had been determined chosen as the place of contest, So I went to that place. The place of contest was a broad space which is covered with short thick grass. The spectators who stood on the hills along the place were very numerous.

First game I saw was "Catching flags". Some flags which were colored to various colors were planted at one end of the arena, and the students took places at the opposite end, and at a given signal

Composition.

    4 th class.
    M. Ōtani

   the
About ∧ Gymnastic Contest of Last
    Saturday.

I could not play myself at the gym-
nastic=contest of last Saturday, be-
courss I have hurt my heart a little.
Therefore I will write down about the
playings which I saw ~~in~~ <*at*> it.
 The weather was very fine for October,
       the
and it was <*a*> very good day for ∧ contest.
I went to my school at eight o'clock
in the   *had*
~~at~~ morning, but all my friends ~~was~~
     had been
started Ninomal which ~~was~~
 chosen
~~determined~~ as the place of contest. So
I went to that place. The place of
    a   *space*
contest was ∧ broat <*d*> ~~turf which is~~ covered
with short thick grass. The spectator<*s*>
who stood on the hills along the
place w~~as~~<*ere*> very numerous.
The
∧ First game I saw was "Catching flags."
       of
Some flags which w~~as~~<*ere*> ~~colored to~~ various
colors were planted at one end of the
       their
arena, and the students took ∧ places
       given
at the opposite end, and at a ∧ ~~giv~~ signal

  ri (?)

作文

  4組
  大谷 M.

先週土曜日の運動会
  について

私は先週土曜日の運動会には少しばかり心臓の具合がよくなかったので参加できませんでした。ですからそこで見学した競技について書いてみたいと思います。天気は10月としてはとても良く、運動会には最適の日でした。朝の8時に学校に行きましたが友だちは皆会場となる二の丸広場に向かっており、私もその場所に行きました。会場は背丈の低い草で厚く覆われている広い場所で、大勢の観客が周囲の小高い高台から眺めて見ていました。最初の競技は「旗取り」でした。さまざまな色の旗が運動場の一方の端に立てられ、生徒たちはその反対側に陣取って、合図の号砲が鳴ると

—sound of gun — the students started at full speed toward the flags, and having reached to the place where little flags were planted, each students snatched one, and ran back to their places at same speed, and the first to get back was the conqueror. This prize was paper, I suppose. Next was Tug=of=war which players was the students of the primary school belonged to the normal school. A great number of students divided themselves into two bands, and one band took the hold of one end of a rope; and the other band took the hold of the other end. Then at a given signal, the two bands, facing each other, pull the rope in different directions with all their might, and a party who succeeded to pull the other over a line drawn between them was winner. This playing's prize was drawing-paper. The next was footrace

− sound of gun − the students started at full speed toward the flags, and ~~on~~ having reached ~~to~~ the place where <*the*> little flags were planted, each students snatched one, and ran back to ~~his~~ *their* places at <*the*> same speed, and the first to get back was the conqueror.   This prize was paper, I suppose.   Next was Tug=of=war which players ~~was~~<*ere*> the students of <*the*> primary school belong~~ed~~<*ing*> to ∧ *the* normal school. A great number of students divided themselves into two bands, and one band took the hold of one end of a rope; and the other band took the hold of the other ~~ban~~ end. Then at a given signal, the two bands, facing each other, pull<*ed*> the rope in different directions with all their might, and ~~a~~ <*the*> party who succeed<*ed*> ~~to~~ <*in*> pull<*ing*> the other ~~ovr~~ over a line drawn between them was winner. This~~e~~<*e*>~~playing~~~~'s~~ ~~for~~ prize ∧ *for this contest* was drawing-paper. The next ∧ *game* was ∧ *a* footrace

[21]   About the Gymnastic Contest of Last Saturday   先週土曜日の運動会について

hat was played by our middle school students. About twenty students were selected from the various class to take part, and he who succeeded to run about 400 yards was the conqueror. All players of footrace had the special hats (caps) which were made of cotton and colored to yellow or black or red or blue. The first winner was Mr. S. Shimidgu who ran in one minute to the place and received twelve volumes of books. The next winner was Mr. Sakane who received the books. Third was Mr. Orito and Mr. Inoue who received the little book(?). The students of all the primary school of Matsuye who was numerated to 1200, conducted the exercise which was called Kiyōei-jitsu. The next was the "picking up the balls." Many little colored balls were scattered here and there, and the students who was the girl of primary

~~that was played~~ <u>made</u> by our middle school's students. About twenty students were selected from the various class<es> to take part, and he who succeeded to run about 400 yards <u>first</u> ∧ was the conqueror. All ~~players of~~ <u>the contestants in the</u> footrace had ~~the~~ special ~~hats~~ <caps> which were made ~~by~~ <of> cotton and colored ~~to~~ yellow or black or red or blue. The first winner was Mr. S. Shimidzu who ran in one minute <to> the ~~place~~ <u>goal</u> and received twelve volumes of book<s>. <The> next winner was Mr. Sakane who received ~~the~~ books. <The> third was Mr. Orito and Mr. Inoue who received ~~the~~ little book<s>(?). The students of all <the> primary school<s> of ~~mat~~ Matsuye ~~who was numerated to~~ <u>numbering about</u> 1200, ~~conducted~~ <u>performed</u> the exercise which ~~was~~ <u>is called</u> Kiyōsei=jitsu. ∧<u>The</u> Next ∧<u>game</u> was ~~the~~ "picking up the balls." Many, little & colored balls were scattered here and there, and the ~~students~~ <u>contestants</u> who ~~was~~ ∧<u>were</u> ~~the~~ <u>the</u> girl<s> of ∧<u>the</u> primary

約20人の生徒がいろいろなクラスから選ばれて参加し、距離にして約400ヤードを一番で走った人が勝者となります。「かけっこ」の参加者は全員木綿でできた丸型の特別の帽子をかぶっていました。その色は黄、黒、赤、青のいずれかでした。一着は清水君でゴールまで1分で走って本を12冊もらいました。二着は坂根君で書物を数冊貰いました。三着は折戸君と井上君で小さな本(?)を貰いました。1200人にものぼる松江の小学校の生徒たちは全員矯正術と呼ばれる体操をしました。次の競技は「玉拾い」でした。たくさんの小さな色つきの玉があちこちばら撒かれており、小学校の女子生徒が

[21] About the Gymnastic Contest of Last Saturday　先週土曜日の運動会について　99

school, started at a given signal, and she who picked up the yellow and red and white balls, and reached to a determined place quickly, was winner. Prize was book, I think. Next was "Three men four feet." The three men faced in one direction, and the party who binded neighbored feet, and ran to a place, and seized the little flag, and returned to their own place came winner. This same playing has been played by the normal school's students. And after two games, there was "Pulling down flags" that was played by the students of Shinsin=gakkuan, a private school of Matsuye. There were two flags which was planted in the arena about 100 yards apart; and two bands of students each numbering about thirty contestants, formed themselves into parties of attack and defence. The left foot of the outer man was tied to the right foot of the middle man & the left foot

school, started at a given signal, and she
who
∧ picked up the yellow and red and
                    first
white balls, and ∧ reached ~~to a deter-~~
         the   *appointed*
~~mined~~ ∧ place ~~fast~~ ~~quickly~~, was winner. Prize was book, I think. Next was "Three men four feet." The three
            faced in
men ~~arranged to~~ one direction, and
                    the party who
~~binded neighbored feet~~, and ∧ ran
to a place, and seized the little
flag, and returned to their own
       first   *game*
place ∧ w<ere> winners. This ~~playing~~
                 the
~~was has been~~ <*was*> played by ∧ normal
school's students.   And after
two games, there was "Pulling
down flags" that was played by
the students of Shinsin=gakkuan,
a private school of Matsuye.
There ~~was~~<*ere*> two flags which was planted
in the arena about 100 yards
apart; and two bands of students
              to
each numbering ∧ about thirty
contestants, formed themselves into
parties of attack and defence.

the left foot of the outer man was tied to the right
foot of the middle man & ~~the left foot of~~ —

合図とともに走り出して黄や赤や白の玉を拾って早く目的地にたどり着いた者が勝者となります。賞品は本だったと思います。次の競技は「三人四脚」です。三人は一緒に前方の同じ一方向に向かって走ります。そして隣の人と足を結び、所定の所まで走り、小さな旗を取って元のところに一番先に戻ったグループが勝者となります。このゲームは師範学校の生徒が行うものでした。そしてこれを2ゲーム行なった後で「旗倒し」が行なわれました。これは松江の私立学校進取学館の生徒によるものです。運動場の両端に約100ヤード離して旗を二本立てます。一グループ約30人の生徒のグループが二つできて攻撃と防衛の二手に分かれます。

外側の人の左足は中の人の右足に結び、そして左足―

編者注：松江八雲会の村松眞吾氏によれば「shinsin＝gakkuan」は修道館の前身の私立学校「進取学館」であろうとのこと。

The band who could bend down the enemy's flag to the ground was conqueror.

And after 10 games there was fencing of the kings called Kawarake-uchi. It was played by our academy's students. Two bands which numbered 80 men were placed to places distant about 70 yards apart. The object of the contest was to attack the symbol which was tied to the arms. The prize was books. Other games the students of 1st class of our school exerted the "Tug-of-war". Above game was played in the forenoon. In the first game of afternoon there was "burning the castle". Two castles which were made of wood were erected in opposite place.

If the drug which was placed on the summit of castle was upset, the fire

The band who ~~bend~~ *could* bend down the enemy's flag to the ground was conqueror.

And after 10 games there was ~~a~~ *some* fencing ~~that is~~ *of the kind* called Kawarake = uchi. It was played by our academy's students. Two bands which ~~was~~ numbered ~~to~~ 80 men ~~was~~<ere> ~~placed~~ *took their* ~~to two~~ places ~~distant~~ *apart* about 70 yards. ~~It was this playing~~ *The object of the contest was* to ~~attack~~ *strike* the symbol which was tied to the arms. The prize was books. After other games the students of <the> 1st class of our school ~~exerted the~~ *had a* "Tug = of = war." ~~Above playing~~ *All the games* ~~was~~<ere> ~~exerted~~ *played* in ~~before noon~~ *the forenoon game*. In the first *the* of *the* afternoon, ~~there~~ was "burning ~~out~~ the castle." Two castles which were made ~~by~~<of> wood were ~~elee~~ erected in opposite place<s>.

If the ~~medicine~~ *drug* which was placed on the summit of castle was ~~turned upside down~~ *upset*, the fire

敵の旗を地面に倒した方が勝になります。これを10ゲームやった後でカワラケ－ウチと呼ばれる剣道の試合があります。これは我が校の生徒が行います。一グループ80人を擁する二つのグループが約70ヤード離れて陣取ります。目的は腕に付けた標（しるし）をアタックすることです。賞品は書物でした。他の競技の後、我が校の一年生の生徒による「綱引き」がありました。午前中の競技は全部終りましたが昼からのゲームのはじまりは「城落し」でした。木で作った二つの城が互いに相対して建てられます。もし城の頂上に置かれた薬品がまっ逆さまに落ちたら

[21]　About the Gymnastic Contest of Last Saturday　先週土曜日の運動会について　103

△ ~~whichever side first had~~ their castle ~~was~~ burned it will ~~be fair.~~ lost the contest.

old
will ~~arose~~ arise instantly.
The two bands picked up the little balls which ~~was~~ scattered ~~to~~ about, and ~~stroke for~~ threw them at the summit. △ In this ~~time~~ game the South ~~was failed.~~ lost.
After many other games, the students of ~~the~~ 2nd year of my middle school conducted the "Pulling down the flags." This prize was stockings. There was a "hurdle race" also. Upon the race-track many obstacles were placed. The first obstacle was a ~~shelf.~~ thing.
Second was a straight line over which we ~~was necessity~~ under were obliged to jump.
Third was a barrier over which we had to climb. Fourth was a little bridge which was made of smooth and round wood.
Fifth was a sort of maze through which we had to crawl on hands and knees. The first conqueror in my school was

whichever side first had
△ If their castle ~~was~~ burned ~~it will be fail~~. <lost the contest.>

~~was~~<ould> ~~arose~~ arise instantly.
The two bands picked up the little
ball<s> which ~~was~~<ere> scattered ~~to~~ <about>,
   threw them at
and ~~stroke for~~ the summit. △ In
    game the   lost
this ~~time~~, ∧ south ~~was failed~~.
After many other games, the students
of ~~two~~ 2nd year of my middle
school conducted the "Pulling
down the flags. This prize was
stockings. There was <a> "hurdle
race" also. Upon the race-track
many obstacles were placed.
                     a fence
<The> First obstacle was ~~shelf~~.
<The> Second was a straight line over
        ~~under~~   *were obliged*
which we ~~was~~ ∧ ~~necessity~~ to jump.
<The> Third was a barrier over which
we had to climb. <The> Fourth was a
little bridge which was made
~~by~~<of> smooth and round wood.
<The> fifth was a sort of maze through
which we had to crawl on
hands and knees. The first
conqueror in my school was

どちらの側にしても
△もし城が先に落ちた方が負けです。

その瞬間火が上がることになっています。両グループは辺りにばら撒いてある小さなボールを拾って頂上めがけて投げるのです。△この競技では南軍が敗けました。他の多くの競技の後、我が中学の2年生が「旗倒し」をやりましたが、このときの賞品はストッキングでした。また「障害物競走」もありました。走路にはたくさんの障害物が置いてあり、最初の障害は垣根（フェンス）でした。二つ目は真っ直ぐに張られた綱で、その上を飛び越えて行きます。第三番目はよじ登って越えてゆく柵、四番目は丸くて滑りやすい小さな橋で、五番目は一種の迷路でそこを腕と膝を使って通過しなければなりません。
我が校の優勝者は

[21] About the Gymnastic Contest of Last Saturday　先週土曜日の運動会について　105

Mrs. I. Kadowaki who received the red blanket and ~~a~~ thirty ~~papers of news~~ newspapers named ~~Matsuye Dailynews~~, Matsuye=Daily=news. After other many ~~playings~~ games, the students of Matsuye-higher-primary-school ~~exerted~~ performed an exercise with dumb-bell which ~~was~~ made of wood. It was very beautiful playing. And after other many games, the contest was finished, and all the students who attended the contest sang the song that prays for the immortality of Our Great Sacred Emperor. When I returned to my house, it was ~~best~~ time for ~~a~~ the supper already.

Fourth class.

M. Otani

"many otter" is better than "otter many"

Mr. I. Kadowaki who received the
red blanket and ~~##~~ thirty ~~papers~~
newspapers
~~papers of news~~ named ~~Matsue-daily news~~ *ye*
Matsuye = Daily = news.　After
　　　　　　　　　games
other many ~~playings~~, the students
of Matsuye-higher-primary-
　　　　　performed
school　~~exerted~~　an exercise
with dumb-bell<s> which ~~was~~<*were*> made
~~by~~ <*of*> wood.　It was very beautiful playing.　And after other
*many games, the contest
was finished, and all the
　　　　　　　　　the
students who attended ∧ contest
sang the song that prays
for the immortality of
Our Great Sacred Emperor.
When I returned to my house,
it was ~~best~~ time for ~~##~~ the
supper already.
　　　　　　　　Fourth class.
"many other" is 　　M. Ōtani
better than
"other many"

門脇君で赤い毛布と松江日日新聞三十枚を貰いました。その後にも多くの競技があって、松江高等小学校の生徒たちが木でできたダムベルで体操をしました。これはとても見事なものでした。他に多くの競技＊があって、運動会は終わりました。そしてこの運動会に参加した生徒は全員で偉大で神聖な天皇の不滅を願う歌を歌いました。帰宅したらもう夕食の時間になっていました。

　　　　　　　　　　　　　4組
"other many"よりも　　大谷　M.
"many other"の方が
良い

[21]　About the Gymnastic Contest of Last Saturday　先週土曜日の運動会について　107

Dear Mr. Otani:—

Please do not make your compositions so long. Your teacher has a great many to correct; and long compositions he has no time to correct. Also it is better for all of you to write short compositions for the present.

Lafcadio Hearn

(Very good)

Dear Mr. Otani:—

Please do not make your compositions so long. Your teacher has a great many to correct; and long compositions he has no time to correct. Also it is better for all of you to write short compositions for the present.

Lafcadio Hearn

———

(Very good)

大谷君へ：—

どうか作文をこんなに長くしないで欲しい。先生は添削する作文の数がとても多いので長文を添削する時間がありません。また差し当りは短いものを書いてくれるとありがたいのだが。

ラフカディオ・ハーン

————————

（とてもよく出来ている）

[22] The Centipede　百足

Composition.
　　　　4.　　M. Otani
　　The Centipede.
I do not ~~kow~~ know any particular fact about the centipede.
The centipede is a many legged insect, and its body consists ~~with~~ of many joints. ~~He~~ It lives in the wall. ~~His~~ Its crawling is very ugly. Many birds pick up ~~them~~ centipedes and give them to their ~~children~~ young ones as ~~the~~ sweet food. ~~He~~ The Centipede is used as an important medicine. The man who(*) inhabits ~~in~~ a great house and ~~worn~~ wears beautiful clothes and does not ~~make~~ do some ~~advantage~~ service to ~~their~~ his country is inferior ~~than~~ to the centipede.

It would be better to say "lives in a great house."

In speaking of animals, we say in English "their young ones" instead of "their children." — Except in the case of animals of which the young have special names, — such as "kitten" "puppies" "chicken" &c.

Composition.

4.   M.Otani

The Centipede.

I do not ~~kow~~ know any particular fact about the centepede.
The centipede is ∧*a* many legged insect, and its body consists ~~with~~ *of* many joints. ~~He~~ <*It*> lives o<*i*>n the wall. ~~His~~ <*Its*> crawling is very ugly.
Many birds pick up ~~them~~ *centipedes* and give ~~them~~∧*to their* ~~children~~ *young ones* as ~~the~~ sweet foods. ~~He~~∧*The centipede* is used as an important medicine.
The man who* inhabits ~~in~~ <*a*> great house and ~~worn~~ <*wears*> beautiful clothes and does not ~~make~~ *do* ∧some ~~advantage~~ *service* to ~~the~~ his country, is inferior ~~than~~ ∧*to the* the centipede!

* It would be better to say "<u>lives in a great house.</u>"

In speaking of animals, we say in English "their young ones" instead of "their children." – Except in the case of animals of which the young have special names, – such as "kittens" "puppies" "chickens" etc.

作文

4. 大谷 M.

百足

私は百足のことについては特に何も知らない。百足は多足の虫でその体躯は多くの関節から出来ている。住んでいる場所は壁の中でその這いまわる姿はとても醜い。鳥の多くは百足を捕えては雛にご馳走として与える。百足はまた大切な薬として使われる。大きな家に住み、きれいな服を着ていても国に奉仕しない人は百足よりも劣っている！

"<u>lives</u> in a great house" といった方がよい。

動物については―たとえば「子猫」「子犬」「ヒヨコ」などのように子供について特別の呼び名を持たない場合―英語では子供の言い方は"children"ではなく"young ones"と言う。

[22] The Centipede 百足 111

[23] How did you spend this summer vacation?　この夏休みをどう過ごしましたか？

to spend, –spent,– spending.– *(pencil correction: perfect)*

Composition.

5th year　M. Ōtani

How did you spend this summer vacation?

Once I said to you that I ~~will~~ *would* take a journey through <u>Idzumo-no kuni</u> to collect ~~the~~ plants and insects for specimens of natural history, as soon as I ~~have~~ *had* passed our fourth class. And, according to this word, I took a ~~travel~~ *journey* at first toward <u>Ōda</u>, which is a city ~~in~~ *at* the north-west ~~bottom~~ *side* of <u>Sanbe</u> mountain, *the very next day after* ~~from next day~~ of graduation ceremony. The object of this trip was to ascend the Volcano of <u>Sanbe</u>, to see its extinct crater, and to collect volcanic plants. I arrived ~~to~~ *at* <u>Ōda</u> *on the* at 20th day of July. But all those days having been very rainy, I could not ascend, and returned home without obtaining any things.

<u>*perfect*</u>

to spend, − spent, − spending.

Composition.

5th year M. Ōtani

How did you spent <*d*> this summer vacation?

       would

Once I said to you that I ~~will~~ take a journey through <u>Idzumo-no kuni</u> to collect ~~the~~ plants and insects for specimens of natural

     had

history, as soon as I ~~have~~ passed our fourth class. And, accord-

      journey

ing <*to*> this word, I took a ~~travel~~ at first toward <u>Ōda</u>, which is

 at   *side*

a city ~~in~~ the north-west ~~bottom~~ of

     the very next day after

<u>Sanbe</u> mountain, ~~from next day~~ of graduation ceremony. The object of this trip was to ascend the

   of

Volcano ∧ <u>Sanbe</u>, to see its extinct crater, and to collect volcanic

     at *on the*

plants. I arrived ~~to~~ <u>Ōda</u> ~~at~~ 20th day of July. But all those days having been very rainy, I could not ascend, and <*re*>turned home without obtaining any things.

          <u>完了形</u>

       to spend, − spent, − spending

        作文

        5年　大谷 M.

この夏休みを
どうすごしましたか？

以前、4年生の過程が終わったらすぐに博物学上の種を求めて植物や昆虫を採集するのに<u>出雲の国</u>を旅すると言ったことがありました。そしてこの言葉通り卒業式の次の日に三瓶山の北西にある<u>大田</u>の町にまず行きました。この旅行の目的は死火山となった火口を見、火山植物を採集するために三瓶山に登ることでした。<u>大田</u>には7月20日に着きました。しかしその日は終日雨で山には登れず、何も得るものもなく家に帰りました。

[23]　How did you spend this summer vacation?　この夏休みをどう過ごしましたか？

Next, I ascended to the summit of Daisen which is the highest mountain in the Sanindo, with Mr. B. Nagasaki, on the 26th day. I visited many ruined temples on the mountain. The view from this mountain was very very good. I collected many rare species of butterflies (Lepidoptera). Next, on the second day of August, I went to a village called Kumano where there is a famous shrine. In that shrine, I saw many plates, drinking cups, looking glasses, and swords used in old Japan. This village is 7 miles distant from Matsue. Near a waterfall of this village I collected many curious ferns (Filicineae), and mosses (Bryophyta). Next, on the 17th day, I went to a Buddhist temple in Kamo village, and staying in this temple I

Next, I ascended to the summit of
Daisen which is the highest
mountain in <*the*> Sanindō, with Mr.
B. Nagasaki, ~~at~~ *on the* 26th day. I
visited many ruined temples ~~in~~ *from*
on the mountain. The view ~~in~~
this mountain was very very good.
I collected many rare species
of butterflies (Lepidoptera). Next,
~~at~~ *on the* second day of August, I went
to a village ∧ *called* Kumano where there
is a famous shrine. In that
shrine, I saw many plates, drinking
cups, looking glasses, and swords
used in old Japan. This village
is 7 miles ~~far~~ *distant* from Matsue.
Near a waterfall of this village I
Collected many curious ferns
(Filicineae), and mosses (Bryophyta).
Next, ~~at~~ *on the* 17th day, I went to a
Buddhist temple in Kamo village,
and staying in this temple I

次に、26日には山陰道で一番高い大山の頂上に長崎君と登りました。私は山上の廃墟になった寺を多く訪ねました。この山からの眺望はとてもとてもよかったです。私はとても珍しい種類の蝶を採集しました。次に、8月2日に有名な神社のある熊野という村に行きました。この神社では昔の日本で使われていたたくさんの皿、盃、鏡、刀剣などを見ました。この村は松江から7マイルのところにあります。この村の滝の近くで私は珍しい羊歯や苔を採集しました。次に、私は17日には加茂村のお寺に行き、この寺に滞在して

[23] How did you spend this summer vacation? この夏休みをどう過ごしましたか？

examined some Buddhist books.
investigated Buddhist books very little.

Above is the simple journal of my summer vacation this year.

AT. — Exact time and place.
ON. — Used before dates of days and nights
IN. — "   "   "   " weeks, months, years &

In speaking of *or near* present time, the preposition IN need not be used.
Examples:— "Today is the 1st."
"Tomorrow will be fine."
"Yesterday I saw him."
No preposition { "This week is a busy week."
"This month is cold."
"This autumn is cool."
"This year there are many storms."

examined some Buddhist books.
~~investigated Buddhist books very little.~~

<A>bove is the simple journal of ^*my* summer vacation ~~in~~ this year.

AT. — Exact <u>time</u> and <u>place</u>.
ON. — used before dates of <u>days</u> <u>and</u> <u>nights</u>
IN. — 〃　〃　〃　〃 weeks, months, years etc.

In speaking of present ^or near time the preposition IN <u>need not be used</u>.
　　Examples: — "Today is the 1st."

No preposition
{
"Tomorrow will be fine."
"Yesterday I saw him."
"This week is a busy week."
"This month is cold."
"This autumn is cool."
"This year there are many storms."
}

ほんの少しばかりの仏教書を調べました。
　上に書いたことは私の今年の夏休みの簡単な日記です。

AT. — 厳密な時間と場所。
ON. — 昼夜の日付の前に用いられる。
IN. — 週、月、年の前に用いられる。

現在あるいは近接の時間のことを表す場合前置詞 IN <u>は使う必要はない</u>。
　例: — "Today is the 1st."
　　　(今日は最初の日です。)

前置詞は不要
{
"Tomorrow will be fine.
(明日は晴れるでしょう。)"
"Yesterday I saw him.
(昨日私は彼に会った。)"
"This week is a busy week.
(今週は忙しい週だ。)"
"This month is cold.
(今月は寒いです。)"
"This autumn is cool.
(今年の秋は涼しい。)"
"This year there are many storms." (今年は嵐が多い。)
}

[23]　How did you spend this summer vacation?　この夏休みをどう過ごしましたか？

【24】 The Owl 梟

Composition.
4th c 5. Atami

The Owl.

The owl is a curious bird. It have very large eyes like those of a cat. During the day, it hides in dark places in the mountains, and in the night it comes out to the village to catch ~~the book~~ its prey ~~to be its~~ ~~eggs~~. Its hooting which is sometimes heard is very dismal. So, its hooting is used as a threat, to make children stop crying ~~to treat the boy is not with~~. Because its voice is heard thus. "O, HO! Sorotto kōka sorotto kōka." It means: ~~Let~~ "Thou! I will enter slowly if ~~you do not~~ thou dost stop the weeping." It is said that if it comes near a house and hook, next day ~~of the~~ night will be very fine. For the reason it is said that its hooting is heard thus. "O, HO! Non inke ho, HO." It means that "Non! make the

Composition.

4th M. Ōtani

The Owl.

The owl is a curious bird. It ha~~ve~~s very large eyes like those of a cat. During the day, it hides in dark places in the mountains, and in the night it comes ⋀*out to the villages* to catch ~~the food to the villages~~ *prey*. Its hooting which is sometimes heard is very dismal. So, its hooting is used ~~to threat the boy to not weep~~ *as a threat to make children stop crying*. Because its voices is heard thus. "Ho! Ho! Sorotto kōka sorotto kōka." It means: ~~that~~ "Thou! I will enter slowly, if ~~you do~~ ⋀*thou dost* not stop the weeping." It is said that if it comes near ~~to~~ a house and hoots, ⋀*the* next day ~~of that night~~ will be very fine. For the reason, it is said that its hooting is heard thus. "H0! Ho! Noritsuke ho, H0." It means that "Thou! make the

作文

4年　大谷 M.

梟

梟は好奇心をそそる鳥です。猫のような大きな目を持っています。日中山の暗いところに隠れていて真夜中になると獲物を獲るために村に出て来ます。時々聞こえるホーホーという鳴き声はとても寂しそうに聞こえます。それでその鳴き声は子供たちを脅かして泣き止ませるのに用いられます。その声は「ホーホー、そろっとこーか、そろっとこーか」と聞こえるので泣き止まないとそろっと入っていくぞという意味になるのです。もしも梟が家の近くにやってきてホーホーと鳴くと次の日は晴れると言われています。そのためにその鳴き声は次のように聞こえます。「ホーホー、のりつけホーホー」その意味は「次の日に

[starch?] Tomorrow

paste to use in washing ~~in the next day.~~ ~~It is by the reason hot~~ For, unless it ~~will~~ be fine, we can not do washing. The owl is ^a very cruel and unfilial bird, and if its parents ~~will be~~ ^are very old and itself feels hungry, it will slay and eat them. Its name in the ~~natural history~~ ~~biology~~ or ornithology (the science of birds) is "Syrnium rufescens."

Biology is the Science of Life — how plants and animals grow and propagate, and why they have special shapes, colors or habits, — and the chemistry of digestion, bloodmaking, etc.

[*starch?*]　　　　　　　*tomorrow*
paste to use in washing ~~in the next~~
　　　　　　　　　　　For
~~day."~~ ~~It is by the reason that~~ ∧ unless
it ~~will~~ be fine, we can not do wash-
　　　　　a
ing. The owl is ∧ very cruel and
unfilial bird, and if its
parents ~~will~~ be<*come*> very old and itself
feels hungry, it will slay and
eat them.　　Its name o<*i*>n ~~the~~
natural history[(1)]
~~biology~~ is "Syrnium rufescens."
　　　or
ornithology
("*the science of birds*")

　　　Biology is the <u>*Science of Life*</u> —
　　　how plants and animals grow
　　　and propagate, and why they
　　　have special shapes, colors,
　　　or habits, — *and the chemistry*
　　　of digestion, bloodmaking, etc.

洗濯する時に糊を使っていいよ」ということなのです。天気が悪ければ洗濯することはできません。梟はとても残酷で親不孝な鳥で、もしその両親が年老いて空腹を覚えたら親を殺して食べてしまいます。その博物学上の名称は"Syrnium rufescens"つまり鳥類学（「鳥の科学」）です。

生物学は<u>生命の科学</u>である。―それは植物や動物がどのように育ち、繁殖するか、またなぜ彼らは特異な形、色、習性を持っているかを調べるもの―しかも消化、造血等の化学なのである。

[25] About the little insects which fly to the lamps at night and burn themselves to death
夜、飛んで灯に入り焼け死ぬ小虫について

AT — hours, minutes, seconds — exact time
ON — days and nights
IN — weeks, months, centuries — or INDEFINITE time such as "in the night-time", "in the day-time"

Composition.

4. M. Otani

About the little insects which fly to the lamps at night and burn themselves to death.

If you will take the trouble to look at care round your lamps on a summer night,[1] you will find innumerable little insects that are dazzled by the light of your lamps and burn themselves to death. You will remember the proverb which your parents often repeated[2] to you in childhood — *Tonde hi ni iru natsu no mushi* (summer insects which fly to fire and place their bodies to death). This proverb has been used as the simile for very very poor things in literary books of Japan. In the present condition of Japan, nearly all Japanese

(2) "Speak" is used only when the words said are not given, or the subject is not mentioned. When the subject is mentioned, then "say" or "tell", or "repeat" is better.

AT – hours, minutes, seconds – what time
ON – days and nights
IN – weeks months centuries – or INDEFINITE time
such as "in the night-time" – "in the day-time"

Composition.
4. M. Ōtani

About the little insects which fly to the lamps at night and burn themselves to death.

If you will take the ~~care round~~ *trouble to look at* your lamps ~~in the~~ *on a* summer night, (1) you will find ~~immence~~ *innumerable* little insects that are ~~dizzied~~ *dazzled* by the light of your lamps and burn themselves to death. You will remember the proverb which your parents often ~~spoke~~ *repeated*(2) to you in ~~the~~ childhood —— Ton de hi ni iru natsu no mushi (~~insects which enter to~~ summer insects which fly to fire and place their bodies to death). This proverb ha~~ve~~<s> been used as the ~~adjectives of~~ *simile* for very very poor things in literary books of Japan. In ∧*the* present condition of Japan, nearly all Japanese

(2) "Speak" is used only when the words said are not given, or the subject is not mentioned. When the subject is mentioned, then "say" or "tell", or "repeat" is better.

AT ―時間、分、秒、―何時
ON ―日中と夜
IN ―週、月、世紀 ― もしくは「夜間」、「日中」
といった不確定な時間

作文
夜、飛んで火に入り焼け死ぬ小虫について
大谷 M. 4.

夏の夜に(1)ランプをよく見るとランプの灯に目がくらんで無数の小さな虫が身を焼いている光景に出くわすことがあります。子供の時親がよく繰り返し言っていた(2)「飛んで灯に入る夏の虫(灯に飛び込んで焼け死ぬ夏の虫)という諺を思い出すことでしょう。この諺は日本の文学書の中では極めて哀れなものの譬えとして用いられています。日本の現況ではほとんど全ての日本人は

(2) "speak"という語は言われた語が示されない場合か主語が現れない場合にのみ用いられる。主語が示される時"say"か"tell"か"repeat"を用いた方が良い。

[25]　About the little insects which fly to the lamps at night and burn themselves to death
　　　夜、飛んで灯に入り焼け死ぬ小虫について

Composition.

5th M. Ōtani

At last composition day, I said that the subject of <u>Kamakiri</u> is very difficult, because I have no particular ~~thing to write~~ facts about it. "Select any subject you like", you said. Then I will write down about "An autumn walk."

~~The~~ Walking in the fields and lanes, particularly on autumn days, is very ~~able~~ good to strengthen our physique. It is true that the smiling spring is more attractive and pleasant than the grave autumn. ~~At~~ In the present season, we can not hear the sweet songs of the <u>uguisu</u>, nor can we smell the enticing fragrance of the cherry-blossom, which is called "the queen of all flowers in Japan." But it is very pleasant to walk in the cool morning, when the silver

Composition.

     5th M. Ōtani

At last composition day, I said
that the subject of Kamakiri is
very difficult, because I ha<d>ve no
   facts about it
particular thing to write. "Select
any subject you like," you said.
Then I will write down about
"An autumn walk."
The w<W>alking in the fields and lanes,
particularly on autumn days, is
  good
very able to strengthen our
physique. It is true that the
smiling spring is more attractive
and pleasant than the grave
   In the
autumn. At present season, we
can not hear the sweet songs of the
    we
uguisu, nor can ∧ smell the entic-
     the
ing fragrance of ∧ cherry-blossoms
which is called the queen of all
flowers in Japan. But it is
very pleasant to walk in the
cool morning, when the silver

作文

    5年 大谷 M．

　前回の作文の時間に、カマキリをテーマにすることはカマキリを知らない私にとっては難しすぎると言いました。そしたら、先生が「何でも君の好きなテーマを選ぶといい」と仰ったので、私は「秋の散策」について書こうと思います。

　野原や小道を散策すること、とりわけ秋の日に散策することは、我々の身体を鍛えるのにとてもよいことです。確かにさわやかな春の方が、地味な秋よりも魅力的で心地よい。今の季節は、鶯の美しい鳴き声を聞くこともあるいは日本で花の女王と呼ばれている桜の魅惑的な香りをかぐこともできない。しかし、霧に覆われた東の山から銀色の太陽が昇るとき、朝涼しい時に散歩し、

We speak in English of "the GOLDEN sun", and "the SILVER moon"

sun shines from the eastern mountain which is covered with mist, and to look up at the brilliant moon of August of kinreki, which is called the moon of the fifteenth night.

~~In some~~ One day I went to Rakugan which is a hill one mile distant from Matsue toward the east. The sky was blue and the air was clear. The rice was golden in the fields with pride, as if thinking that, since it had laboured well to produce such a beautiful effect, it had a right to be proud. I thought that we are now in our Spring and flowering-time, and never must be proud. We have many hopes and anticipations; and there are many duties which we ought to perform. If we conduct ourself honestly, with self-reliance, perseverance,

We speak in English of "The GOLDEN sun", and
 "the SILVER moon"

sun shines from the eastern mountain which is covered with mist,
and to look up ∧ the brilliant   [at]
moon of August of kiureki, which
is called the moon of fifteen<th>   [the]
night.
                              One
In some ∧ day I went to Rakuzan
which is a hill one mile distant
from Matsue toward ∧ east. The   [the]
sky was blue and the air was clear.
The rice was golden in the fields
with pride, as if thinking that,
since it had laboured well to
produce such a beautiful effect,
it had a right to be proud.
                              in our
I thought that we are now ∧ Spring
and flowering-time, and never
must be proud. We have many hopes
and anticipations; and there are
many duties which we ought to perform.
If we conduct ourself<ves> honestly,
with self-reliance, perseverance,

英語では「黄金の太陽」そして
「銀色の月」という言い方をする。

十五夜の月と言われる旧暦八月のきれいな
月を見上げるということは楽しいことであ
る。ある日のこと、松江から東の方一マイ
ルの離れたところにある楽山という山にい
きました。空は青く空気はきれいでした。
稲は誇り高く金色の穂をつけていました。
よく働いたからこれだけの稔りをつけたの
だと言わんばかりで、それもそのはずです。
今は春で花の季節ですがけっして得意に
なっているわけではありません。私たちに
は多くの希望と期待があります。そして果
たすべき責任も多いのです。もし私たちが
確固として、また独立心と勤勉さをもって
正直に振舞えば、

[26] Composition: [An Autumn Walk]   作文 : [秋の散策]   127

and industry, though there are many
temptations and conflicts in the
world, we shall surely gain ~~the~~
beautiful success, with ~~the~~ full
fortune and great honour, ~~like~~ ^even
as the rice became ripened.
   "Heaven helps those who
      help themselves."

                    100

and industry, though th<e>re are many temptations and conflicts in the world, we shall surely gain ~~the~~ beautiful success, with ~~the~~ full *even* fortune and great honour, ~~like~~ as the rice became ripened.

"Heaven helps those who help themselves."

多くの誘惑や葛藤があるけれども私たちはきっと見事な成功を果たし財産も栄誉も手に入れることができるでしょう。それは稲が豊かに稔るようなものなのです。
　『天は自ら助くる者を助く』

判読・復元・日本語訳

「田辺勝太郎」の英作文添削

The Compositions of Tanabe Katsutaro

Rice.

K. Tanabe.

There are very numerous species of ~~vegetables~~ *nutritive plants* in the world,—~~as~~ *such* rice, barley, wheat, oats, peas, etc. But we prefer rice to the rest; because it is the chief staple, or cereal in Japan, being the national food for the people from ~~the~~ ancient times down to the present day.

Indeed, the soil and the climate are so ~~much suitable~~ *well adapted* for rice that, wherever we go, rice-fields may be cultivated ~~at~~ *with* ease.

We must, therefore, thank ~~for~~ the bounty of nature; ~~side~~ *for* we owe ~~many~~ *a great deal* to rice.

(good)

~~The~~ Rice.

K. Tanabe

There are very numerous species of ~~nourishable vegetation~~ *nutritive plants* in the world, —∧ *such* as rice, barley, wheat, oat<s>, pea<s>, etc. But we prefer rice to the rest, because it is the chief staple, or cereal in Japan, being the nat~~h~~ional food for the people from ~~the~~ ancient times down to the present day. Indeed, the soil and the climate are so ~~much suitable~~ *well adapted* for rice that, wherever we go, rice-fields may be cultivated ~~at~~ ∧*with* ease. We must, therefore, thank ~~for~~ this bounty of nature, ~~while~~ ∧*for* we owe ~~many interests~~ ∧*a great deal* to rice.

(good)

米

田辺 K.

世界には、稲、大麦、小麦、からす麦、エンドウ豆、などといった栄養価の高い植物の種が数多く存在している。しかしながら、我々は他の何よりも米を好む。理由は米は主要穀物であり、日本では太古の昔から現在まで人々の国民的な食物になってきたからである。実際のところ、土壌や気候は稲によく適しており、行く所どこでも容易に田んぼを耕すことができる。したがって、我々は大いに米のおかげをこうむっている以上この豊かな自然の恵みに感謝しなくてはならない。

（よろしい）

【28】The Seven Deities of Good Fortune 七福神

The Seven Deities of Good Fortune.
5th class. K. Tanabe.

There are the six gods and one goddess of good luck, or of wealth, called the Shichifukujin,— which means the seven deities of good fortune,— in Japan. They are worshipped in a toko or in a household shrine, and on the pictures or on the images, by those who pray for wealth, a peace, a safety, a loveliness, and any other happiness;— or the pictures of them, it is said, are put under the beds, on the 2nd of January, by those who desire to have good and happy dreams.

(good)

The Seven Deities of Good Fortune.
5th class, K. Tanabe.

There are the six gods and ~~the~~ one goddess of good luck, or of wealth, called The Shichifukujin,- which means the seven deities of good fortune,- in Japan. They are worshiped in a toko or in a household shrine, and on the pictures or on the images, *by those who pray for wealth* ~~praying for a //// rich~~ ∧, a peace, a *any* safety, a loveliness, and ~~all~~ other happiness ;— or the pictures of them, it is said, are put //// under the *by those who* beds, on the 2nd of January, ~~by the some~~, desir~~ing~~ to have ~~a~~ good and happy dream<s>.

(good)

七福神

5組　田辺 K.

日本には、福と富をつかさどる六人の神と一人の女神がおり、七福神と呼ばれています。七福神は、日本では七人の福の神という意味です。彼らは、床や神棚に祀られており、富、平和、安全、美、そしてその他あらゆる幸せを祈願する人々によって絵画や彫像の形で崇拝されています。その七福神の絵についての謂れがあり、一月二日にベッドの下にその絵を置いて寝ると良い夢をみることができるのというのです。

（よろしい）

[29] The Frog 蛙

The Frog.

5th Class. K. Tanabe.

The Frog is a common small amphibious reptile, which is skilful in swimming and leaping, and which always lives in the fields, farms, or groves. There are many kinds of this creature; ~~Its sorts are so many that it may be numbered~~ perhaps, at least thirty or forty, and some live for three or four years, and some for twenty or thirty. This animal is often much hurt by the sport of mischievous boys. But it is, I think, one of the most interesting and important animals, because it ~~deserves to drive out~~ away, many hurtful worms or insects ~~privately~~. This is proved from the following facts: it continues to catch various worms in rice-fields, in order to make the stalks grow maturely. This is a very important matter, especially in our country where the ~~usual~~ principal food

<The> Frog.
5th Clags. K. Tanabe.

<The> Frog is a common small amphibious reptile, which is skilled <ful> in swimming and leaping , and which always lives in the fields, farms, or grooves.

There are many kinds of this creature, ~~Its sorts are so many that it may be~~ ~~numbered~~ perhaps, ~~in~~ <at> ∧*least* thirty or forty, and some live for three or four years, and some for twenty or thirty. This animal is ~~always~~ much hurt <in> ~~by~~ ∧*often* sports of mischievous boys. But it is, I think, one of the most interesting and important animals, because it ~~deserves to~~ drive<s> ~~out~~ ∧*away* many hurtful wa<o>rms or insects ~~privately~~. This is proved from the following ~~facts:~~ *the* it continues to catch various worms in rice-fields , in order to make the stalks grow~~n~~ maturely.

This is ∧*a* very important matter, especially in our country where the ~~usual~~ food
principal

蛙

5組　田辺 K.

蛙はたいていは小さい両生類の爬虫類です。それは泳ぐことや跳ねることがうまく、普段は野原や農場や溝の中に住んでいます。この生き物はおそらく少なくとも30種か40種あって、3年か4年の寿命のものもおれば、20年か30年も生きるものもいます。この生き物はよくいたずら好きな少年たちに弄ばれて痛めつけられます。しかし、蛙は一番興味深く、大切な生き物だと私は思います。というのは蛙は有害な虫や昆虫を駆除してくれるからです。このことは以下の事実で証明されています。つまり、蛙はいつも虫を捕まえて稲の茎を十分成長させてくれます。これは特に、主食が米である我が国にあっては、とても重要なことなのです。

of the people is nice. The Tree-frog, which has a green back and a white belly, feeds on many mischievous worms in the various kinds of fruit-trees. And the toad, though its appearance is very awkward, deserves also the same important consideration. Thus we have to acknowledge that the frog is a very respectable animal at an agricultural point of view, and therefore that it is very wrong to hurt it for mere sport.

of the people is rice. The Tree-frog, which has a green
back and a white belly, feeds
on many mischievous worms in
the various kinds of fruit-trees. And <the>
toad, though its appearance is very
awkward, deserves also the same
consideration. Thus we have to
acknowledge that the frog is a very repect-
able animal f<rom> the agricultural
point of view, and therefore that it is
very wrong to hurt it for <mere>
sport.

アマガエルは背中が緑色でお腹が白く、様々な種類の果樹に付く害虫を食べてくれます。そしてヒキガエルは、見かけはとても不格好だが、同様に考えられます。このように私たちは蛙が農業の観点からもっと大切にされて然るべき生き物であり、だからこそ蛙をただの気晴らしで痛めつけることなどはあってはならないことだということを理解しなければなりません。

[29] The Frog 蛙 139

The Most wonderful Thing.

5th K. Tanabe.

What is the most wonderful thing in this world we have ever seen or heard of? It is hardly too much to say that it must be water. Rain purifies the air that is being habitually rendered unfit to breathe by us, and wets the ground to prevent the earth from being too much scorched by the sun by day; the rivers provide the water-animals, which furnish us with a good dinner, with food, and the vegetable kingdom with manure; and the ocean supplies us with food, medicine and many materials for arts and manufactures, and affords us most excellent means of communication, which may extend mutual knowledge to other countries.

Mrs. G. Wilson says "the most wise of active nations are those which dwell in countries richly provided with water". Indeed, the primitive seats of human society was the alluvial basins of the Nile, of the

The Most ~~extraordinary~~ *wonderful* Thing.

5~~th~~ K. Tanabe.

What is the most ~~extraordinary~~ *wonderful* thing ~~in this world~~ we have ever seen or heard of ∧ It is hardly too much to say that it must be ~~the~~ water. Rain purifies the air that is being habitually rendered unfit to breathe by us, and wets the ground to ~~protect~~ *prevent* the earth from being too much scorched by the sun by day ; the river provide the water-animals , ∧ which ~~we may have~~ *furnish us with* a good dinner, with food, and the vegetable kingdom with manure ; and ∧ *the* ocean supplies us with food, medicine and many materials for arts and manufactures, and affords us most excellent means of communication, which may extend mental knowledge ∧ *to* ~~with~~ other countries.

Mr. G. Wilson says "the most ~~wisdom~~ *wise* of active nations are those which dwell in countries rich~~ll~~y provided with water." Indeed, the primitive seats of human society ~~was~~<ere> the alluvial basins of the Nile, of the

Tigris and Euphrates and of the Indus; Grecian and Roman splendors arose really from the physical causes of the Mediterranean; the civilizations of old Japan were brought in by the Sea of Japan, and the modern are by the Pacific; the savages of Africa, we may attribute, if possible, to the deficiency of rain. Thus we safely consider that the water is most wonderful thing, notwithstanding it is the most common, in the world.

Tigris and Euphrates and of the Indus; Grecian and Roman splendors arose really from the physical causes of the Mediterranean; the civilizations of old Japan were brought in by the Sea of Japan, and the moderns are by the Pacific; the savages *condition* of Africa, we may attribute, if possible, to the deficience of rain. Thus we safely consider that water is most *wonderful* thing, notwithstanding it is the most common, in the world.

チグリス川やユーフラテス川やインダス川などの流域でありました。ギリシアやローマ文明の輝きも実際には地中海の物質的豊かさに由来するものでした。古代日本の文明は日本海によってもたらされました。そして、近代日本の文明は太平洋によってもたらされたのです。アフリカの未開の状態は、雨不足が原因でしょう。このように私たちは世界で最もありふれた物であるにもかかわらず、水が間違いなく最もすばらしい物であると考えるのが妥当だと思うのです。

【31】Wrestling　相撲

Wrestling.

　　　　　　　Fifth year. K. Tanabe

Wrestling is the exercise in which two men struggle for a fall against each other, and in which they try to throw one another down by tripping up. I have learned the following account of wrestling from Japanese history: in the reign of an Emperor Suinin, about 1,750 years ago, there was a strong wrestler named Kuehaya, on the one hand, in Toma, and on the other, Nominosukune who was a native of Kizuki in Izumo, and who now still is worshipped by a many wrestlers, He was also strong. They were ever matched in wrestling by the Emperor, but the former lost and died. This seems to be the origin of wrestling in Japan. From that time this sport became popular everywhere through the various periods to the present day; and it is proved easily by the appearances of wrestlers, which is formidable, that this exercise is very beneficial for

(1) "and it may easily be seen from" — would be better.

Wrestling.

Fifth year, K. Tanabe.

Wrestling is the exercise ∧which ∧struggle [*in*] [*two men*]
for a fall against each other, and ∧which [*in*]
~~through~~ ∧another down by tripping up. [*they try to throw one*]
I have learned ~~ever~~ ∧following account [*the*]
∧from Japanese history: in the reign [*of wrestling*]
of an Emperor Suinin, about 1,750 years
ago, there was a strong wrestler named
Kuehaya, on the one hand, in Toma,
and on the other, Nominosukune who was
a native of Kizuki in Izumo, and who ~~is~~
now still is worship<*ped*> by a many wrestlers,
~~is~~ ∧also strong. They were ever watched in [*He was*]
wrestling by the Emperor, but the former
lost and died. This seems to be the
origin of wrestling in Japan. From that
time this ~~practice~~ ~~prevailed~~ everywhere [*sport*] [*became popular*]
through the various periods to the present
day; <u>and it is proved easily by</u> the ap-
~~pearances~~ of wrestlers, which is formidable,
that this exercise is very ~~interesting~~ ∧for [*beneficial*]

(1) "and it may easily be seen from" — would be better.

相撲

5年，田辺 K.

相撲は、男二人がお互いを倒すことを目的として格闘するスポーツであり、足を掛けて相手を投げ倒すスポーツです。私は、日本の歴史から相撲について次のような逸話を学びました。垂仁天皇の治世、今から1750年くらい前ですが、一方で、当麻のケハヤ(蹶速)という強い相撲取りがおり、また他方で出雲の杵築生まれのノミノスクネ(野見宿禰)という相撲取りがおりました。彼は今でも多くの相撲取りから尊崇されている強い相撲取りでした。2人はかつて天覧試合で戦いましたが前者は負けて亡くなりました。この話が日本の相撲の起源のようです。当時からこの<u>競技</u>は様々な時代を通じて現在まで大いに<u>人気</u>がありました。そして相撲取りは外見は恐ろしく見えますが、この訓練はとても身体に有益であるということは<u>すぐ分かる</u>ことです。

(1)「and it may easily be seen from（〜からすぐ分かる）」の方が良い表現である。

health, but of course the excessive exercise is very ~~wrong for the feeble.~~ injurious to weakly persons —

very good —

health, but of course ~~the~~ excess *ive exercise* ∧ is very ~~wrong for the feebles~~. *injurious to weakly persons.*

very good.

しかしもちろん、過度の訓練は体の弱い人には有害になります。

<u>とてもよろしい。</u>

【32】Letter about Matsue to a friend　友への松江便り

Letter about Matsue
　　　to a friend.　　K. Tanabe.

My dear friend,

　　I will tell you now something about Matsue, the largest and the best city in the Sanindo. There are more than 10,000 houses, than forty thousand population; There are about one hundred splendid streets, in which a government-office, an academic school, a normal school, and a great number of other public buildings, may be seen, and along which, busy traders, mechanics, barbers, buyers and sellers, make their way. On either side of the Ohashi, which means the largest bridge, and which cross the River Ohashi flowing from Lake Shinji into the Nakaumi easterly, the water is nearly filled up with steam-boats and Japanese ships, which afford us excellent means of communication with other cities very much; The

Letter
~~The Information~~ about Matsuye
　　　to a friend.　　K. Tanabe.

My dear friend,
　　　　　tell　　　*something about*
　I will ~~address~~ you now ~~the states~~
~~of~~ Matsuye, the largest and the best city in the
　　　　　　　　are
Sanindo. There ~~the~~ more than 10,000 ~~of the~~
the population is estimated at more
~~human~~ houses, and ∧ than forty thousand ~~////~~
~~of the~~ population, ~~are estimated~~; There
are about one hundred
∧splendid streets, in which a government
office, an academic school, a normal
school, and a great number of other public
buildings, may be seen, and along which,
　　　　　　　　　　　　buyers
busy traders, mechanics, barbers, ~~vendees~~,
　　sellers
and ~~venders~~, make their way, ~~exist on~~
　　　　1
~~about 2 or 3 hundreds~~; o<*O*>n either side
of the Ōhashi, which means the largest
　　　　　which
bridge, and ∧ cross<*es*> the River Ohashi flowing
from ~~the~~ Lake Shinji into the Nakaumi easterly, the water is nearly filled up with
steam-boats and Japanese ships which
afford us excellent means of communication with other cities
~~give us convenience very much~~; The

climate is very mild; literary studies are encouraged; and great attention is paid to trade.
This is all I can tell you, in a general way, about Matsuye.

Your friend
K. Tanabe.

climate is very mild; ~~the~~ literary studies are encouraged; and <*great*> attention is paid ~~zealously on the~~ ^to^ trade.

Th*e*<*i*>s*e* ~~are the information~~ ^*is all I can tell you*^ in a general ~~view,~~ *way,* about Matsuye.

     Your ~~truly~~ friend
     K. Tanabe.

気候は、とても穏やかで、文学の研究が奨励されています。さらに商取引にも重点が置かれています。これが松江について概ね私が今君にお伝えできることのすべてです。

    あなたの真の友
    田辺 K.

【33】Why should we venerate Ancestors? 祖先を敬うべき理由は何か？

Why should we venerate
our Ancestors?
by K. Tanabe.

It has been our proper and general custom to venerate our ancestors, and therefore they are worshipped every day in a household shrine — the Butsudan or the Kamidana. Why should it be so? None of us knows, or has ever tried to know why, because it is the nature of us. In fact, this noble feeling has been inculcated into us without a teacher, and we never thought to examine its reason of it hitherto. However, it can not exist, of course, without any reason. It is, in short, because our ancestors settled the country where we live and our descendants are to live, and all that we enjoy and know was created for us by them, and because they made the condition

Why should we venerate
our Ancestors?
5th K. Tanabe.

It has been our proper and general custom to venerate our ancestors, and therefore they are worshipped every day in a household shrine — the Butsudan or the Kamidana. Why should it be so? ~~Nobody~~ *none* of us knows or ~~attempted~~ *has ever tried* to know why, because it is the nature of us. In fact, this noble feeling has been ~~spread out among~~ *inculcated into* us without a teacher, and we never ~~came~~ *thought* to exa- mine ~~its~~<the> reason ~~hitherto~~ *of it hitherto*. However, it can not ~~be so~~ *exist*, of course, without any reason. It is, in short, because our ancestors ~~established~~ *settled* its country where we live and our descend- ants are to live, and all that we enjoy ~~and know~~ was created for us by them, ~~and~~ because they made the condition

祖先を敬うべき
理由は何か？
5年　田辺 K.

祖先を敬うことは、我々にふさわしく、かつ一般的な慣わしです。したがって、毎日、祖先は家の神棚または仏壇で拝まれている。どうしてそうなっているのか？それは誰にも分からないし、その理由を知ろうと今まで試みても来なかったのです。それは我々にとってごくあたりまえのことだったからです。実際、この崇高な感情は学校の先生によって教えられたのではありません。我々は今までその理由を考え検証することはありませんでした。しかし当然のことながらその理由は必ず存在します。簡単に言えば、我々の祖先は、今我々が生活している場所に定住し、我々の楽しみ、知ることの全てを創造して下さったからなのです。さらに、祖先は

of our household what we now see it.

Extremely good.

of our household what we now see it.

Extremely good.

家庭というものを今あるような姿にして下さったのです。

秀逸である

[34] The fox who borrowed the Tiger's Power　虎の威を借る狐

The fox who borrowed the Tiger's Power.

    5th year, K. Tanabe.

Once upon a time, a tiger and a fox happened to meet at a mountain. Then the tiger was too hungry to miss the chance of eating the fox, and therefore, he soon threatened to eat it by force. At this time, the poor fox cried loudly, striving to hide his fear with a forced air of assurance, "I have descended from heaven as the King of all beasts; therefore if you hurt me ever so little, at once heavy misfortune will certainly befall you." But as the tiger did not believe this, and still wanted to eat him, the fox continued "do you doubt me? then if you come along with me, you will certainly see that, wherever I go all beasts run away for fear of me." Then the tiger assented, thinking of course it could not be so, and, therefore, that he would find an excuse for eating the poor creature.

The fox who borrows<ed> the Tiger's Power.
     5th year, K. Tanabe.

Once upon a time, a tiger and a fox happened to meet at a mountain. Then the tiger was too hungry to ~~pass over~~ ∧*miss the chance of eating* the fox, and therefore, he soon threatened to eat it by force. At this time, the poor fox cried loudly, striving to hide his fear with a forced air of assurance, "I have descended from ~~the~~ heaven as the king of all beasts; therefore if you hurt me ~~very~~ *ever so* little, at once heavy misfortune will certainly befall you." But as the tiger did not believe this, and still wanted to eat ∧*him*, the fox continued "do you doubt me? ~~Then~~ ∧*Then* if you ∧will come along with me, you ∧ certainly see that, wherever I go all beasts run away for fear of me." Then the tiger assented, thinking of course it could not be so, and, therefore, ~~found~~ ##*that he would find an* ~~some~~. ~~Some~~ excuse for eating ~~him~~ *the poor creature.*

~~as affording him an~~
  This is not a mistake but the other is better.

虎の威を借る狐
  5年 田辺K.

昔々、一匹の虎と一匹の狐が山で偶然にも遭遇しました。その時、虎はたいそう空腹だったのでこの機に狐を食べてしまおうと思いました。そこで、虎はこの狐を強引に脅しました。この時、哀れな狐は、この脅しに対して恐怖心を覆い隠すように大声で叫びました。「私は天より使わされた百獣の王である。それゆえ、ほんの少しでも私を傷つけようものならば、たちまち大きな災いがお前に下ろうぞ。」しかしながら、虎は狐の言ったことなど信用せずに、狐を食べてしまいたい一心でした。そこで狐はこう続けました。「お前はこの私を疑うのか？私についてくれば分かるだろうが、私の行く所どこでもあらゆる動物どもは私を恐れて逃げていってしまうぞ。」と。その時、虎はそんなことはありえないと考え、この哀れな生き物を食らう口実を見つけ出そうとしていました。

  ~~as affording him an~~
  これは間違いではないが
  他の言い方の方がよい

At this, they began to walk round, and then the tiger wondered, that wherever they appeared, it resulted just as the fox said, — but it was, in truth, for fear of the tiger, and not of the fox. From this little story, there is a very interesting saying, in Japan, about a man who vaunts himself, acts insolently, and despises others, because of his family's or master's fortune or high position: — "the fox who borrows the tiger's power."

10.0

At this, they began to walk round, and then the tiger wondered *that* wherever *that* they appeared, ~~how~~ it resulted just as the fox said, — but it was, in truth, for fear of the tiger, and not of the fox. From this little story, there is a very interesting saying, in Japan, about a man who vaunts himself, acts insolently, and despises others, ~~from~~ *because of* his family's or master's fortune or ~~eminence~~ *high position*; —— "the fox who borrows the tiger's power."

100

この時、虎と狐は辺りを一緒に歩き始めました。するとその時、虎は自分の目を疑いました。二匹が行くところ何処でも、狐が言った通りになったのでした。しかし、実はそれは虎に対する恐れであって狐に対する恐れではなかったのです。このささやかな物語から、日本では非常に面白い諺が生まれました。自分の家族や上司の財産や社会的に高い立場を利用して、虚勢を張り、横暴に振舞い、他人を軽蔑するような人間のことを「虎の威を借る狐」というようになったのです。

100

The weather of the 15th January

15th K. Tanabe.

In the morning, strange to say, the ground was covered with very deep snow, although last evening was cold, and clear. The sky was very dark with awful masses of clouds; the wind whistled through the whole day, together with frozen flakes which fell more heavily every minute; pools or ponds were frozen up; men were compelled to stay at home; and the ships, which afford us excellent means of communication with other cities, were confined to port by the storm. It was, really, dreadful weather such as we (seldom or rarely) ever saw before.

　　　　　　　　　　the
　　The weather of ∧ 15th Jan<*uary*>.
　　　　　　　　5th, K. Tanabe.

In the morning, strange to say, the ground was covered with ~~the~~ very deep
　　　　　　　although　　*evening*
snow, ~~which the~~ ∧ last ~~night~~ ∧ was ~~though~~
　　and
cold ~~very~~ ∧ clear.　The sky was very dark
　　　　　　　　　　　　　　　the
with ~~the~~ awful masses of clouds; ∧ wind whistled through the whole day, together with ~~the~~ frozen flakes which fell more heavily every minute; pools or ponds were frozen
　　　　　　　　　　　　stay
up; men were compelled to ~~be~~ ∧ at home;
and the
∧ ships, which afford us excellent means of communication ~~wh~~ with other cities, were
confined to port　　　　*really*
~~bound~~ ∧ by the storm. It was, ~~indeed~~, ~~the~~ dreadful weather ~~that we see saw rarely saw before rarely~~ such as we { seldom / or "rarely" } ever saw before.

　　　　　　　１月15日の天候
　　　　　　　　5年　田辺 K.

言うのも変な話ですが、朝、大地がとても深い雪で覆われていました。そもそも、昨晩は寒くそして天気が良かったにもかかわらず。空は、不気味な雲の塊で覆われてとても暗かったのです。風は、一日中ビュービューと唸りながら氷の欠片がより一層激しく、そしてとめどなく降りそそぎ、池や水溜りは凍りついて、人々は家の中でじっとしているほかありませんでした。他の都市を結ぶ、すぐれた交通手段である船は、その嵐のせいで、港に閉じ込められていました。今までめったにお目にかかったことのないような本当に恐ろしい天候でした。

[36] The Tortoise　亀

The Tortoise.

The tortoise is a reptile, armed with a very defensive covering, or shell, under which, when it is attacked by enemy, it can withdraw its head, tail and the limbs.

It, together with the crane, is regarded in Japan, as a sacred animal, and it is said to live for ten thousand years. It is, therefore, one usual custom to use pictures or images of tortoise to celebrate the inaugurations of emperors, or to celebrate the birth day of a man who has reached old age.　K. Tanabe.

articulata is the family to which the division crustacea belongs. The Crustacea have no skeleton properly speak: certain insects and sea-animals such as crabs, lobsters, & shrimp are included in this family. The tortoise belongs to the class of vertebrates, — order "cholonia"

The Tortoise.

The tortoise is ~~an crustacian animal~~ *a reptile*, armed with a very strong ~~weapon~~ *defensive covering*, or shell, under which, when it is attacked by ~~enem~~*its* en*e*mies, it *can* put ~~the~~ *withdraw* its head, ~~the~~ tail and ~~the~~ limbs, ~~in safely~~.

It, together with the crane, is regarded ~~with respect~~, in Japan, as ~~the~~ *a* sacred animal, and it is said to live for ten thousand years. It is, therefore, one usual ~~manner~~ *custom* to use ~~the~~ pictures or ~~the types fo~~ *images* of *celebrate* tortoise to ~~congratulate~~ the inaugurations of ~~the~~ emperors, or to celebrate the birth day of a man who has reached old age.   K. Tanabe.

   <u>Articulata</u> is the family to which the division <u>crustacea</u> belongs. The <u>Crustacea</u> have no skeleton , properly spear: certain insects ##### and sea=nimals such as crabs, lobsters, & shrimp are included in this family. The tortoise belongs to the class of vertebrates, – order *"<u>Cholonia</u>"*

亀

亀はとても頑丈で自分を守るための外皮、つまり甲羅を持った爬虫類である。亀は敵に攻撃された時は甲羅の下に頭、しっぽ、手足を引っ込める。 亀はまた鶴とともに、日本では神聖な生き物と考えられていて、一万年も生きると言われている。それゆえに、天皇の就任を祝ったり、老年に達した人の誕生を祝ったりするのにその絵や像が使われる習慣がある。　　田辺 K.

<u>有関節類</u>は<u>甲殻網類</u>が所属する集団（科）である。<u>甲殻網類</u>は骨格も無ければとげもない；ある昆虫や蟹やウミザリガニや海老などの海洋生物はこの一群に含まれる。亀は脊椎動物の綱、—<u>カメ（ケロニア）</u>目に属する。

編者注：ハーンはカメを表わす chelonia を cholonia と間違って書いたようだ。

【37】The Japanese Spider 日本の蜘蛛

The Japanese Spider.
　　　　　　by Clair K. Tanabe.

The spider is a common small animal which belongs to the Arthropda, and there are so many kinds of this creature, that we can scarcely number them all. The apparent distinction between this creature and any others, is chiefly in the length and number of the legs and the position and arrangement of the eyes; it has always four pairs of legs which have very many joints, and it has, on the whole, eight eyes which are various in arrangement. It weaves skillfully the web which makes it enough home, and by the means of which it may get the food, or insects. There is a very curious saying in Japan:— "The spider which we meet with us at night, by whatever chance, must be slain instantly". We can not understand

The Japanese Spider.
　　　　　　5th Class K. Tanabe.

The spider is a common small animal
which belongs to ^the arthropda, and there
are so ~~many~~ many kinds of this creature,
that we can ~~not~~ scarcely number. <them all.>
The apparent distinction between this creature
　　　　　　　　is
and any others, ~~refers~~ chiefly
　　in
~~on~~ ^ the length and number of the legs
and the position and arrangement of
the eyes: it has always four pairs of
legs which ha~~s~~ <ve> very many joints, and it
has, on the whole, eight eyes which are
various in arrangement.　It weaves
skillfully the web which makes its snug~~ly~~
home, and by the means of which it
may get the food, or insects.　There ~~are~~
is a very curious saying in Japan: —
　　　　　　we meet
"The spider which ~~meets~~ with ~~us~~ at
　　　　by whatever chance
night, ~~however matters~~ , must be slain
instantly". We can not understand

日本の蜘蛛
　　　　5組　田辺 K.

蜘蛛は節足動物門に属するありふれた小さな生き物である。また、この生き物は種類が多いので全ての種類を数え上げることはできない。この生き物と他の生き物を区別するのは主にその足の長さや目の位置や配置によってである。蜘蛛は普通多くの関節を持った四対の足を持ち、だいたいは配列が様々な八つの目を持っている。蜘蛛は自分たちの安全な棲家となる蜘蛛の巣を巧みに織る、そしてこの巣を使って食べ物や虫を捕獲する。日本にはとても不思議な「夜に見た蜘蛛は直ちに殺さなければならない」という諺がある。私たちには

this reason, I think, however, the idea must be very absurd, because the feeds on many mischievous insects and, therefore, it is a very respectable animal from an agricultural point of view.

> I hope you composed all this yourself;— it is so very good that I cannot help thinking you got one or two sentences out of a book.

            of this
the reason ∧. I think, however, the idea
must be very absurd, because ~~he~~<it>
feeds on many mischievous insects
and, therefore, <u>it is a very respectable
animal from an agricultural point
of view.</u>

        *I hope you composed all this
        yourself ; — but it is so very
        good that I cannot help
        thinking you got one or
        two sentences out of a book.*

この理由が分からない。私はこの考えは
とてもおかしいと思う。なぜなら、蜘蛛は
多くの有害な虫を食べてくれるし、それゆ
えに、<u>蜘蛛は農業の観点からはとても大切
にすべき生き物である、</u>と言えるからだ。

君はこれを全て一人で作文したの
だとは思うが、あまり良くできて
いるので先生は君が文を一つか二
つどこかの書物から失敬してきた
のではないかと思わざるをえない
のだが。

【38】To a Bookseller asking for a book　書店に本を注文すること

To a ~~Merchant~~ Bookseller asking for ~~merchandise~~ a book.

Matsue, Decem. 11th, 23. Meiji.

Dear Mr. ——,

there are a great number of "Letter Writers" ~~are~~ in existence; but I complain that the supplies of the most excellent and complete ones, which all students of ~~the~~ our class are extremely desirous to possess, are very ~~little~~ few. If you have any ~~of that~~ good ones in your shop ~~in your shop with good ones~~, which ~~will~~ will be satisfactory to us ~~shall be satisfied with us~~, are kept, please send me ~~the type~~ a copy, and ~~inform~~ let me know the price, immediately, (with both ~~our~~ your and our advantage.

Entirely yours,
K. Tanabe.

"to our mutual advantage" you mean; but you cannot say that in a business-letter.

Bookseller
To a ~~Merchant~~ asking
    a book.
  for ~~Merchandise~~

      11th
Matsue, Decem. ~~11st~~, 23ᵈ, *Meiji*

    Mr. _____
Dear ∧_____,

      are
There ∧ a great number of
"Letter Writ/ers" ~~are~~ in existence; but
I complain that the supplies of the
      complete ones
most excellent and ~~commodious~~ ∧, which
all students of ~~the~~ our class are ex-
    to possess *few*
tremely desirous ∧, are very ~~little~~ . If
you have any good ones in your shop
~~in your shop such good ones~~, which
which will be satisfactory to us
~~shall be satisfied with us~~, are kept,
    a copy
please send me ~~the type~~, and ~~inform~~
let me know
∧ the price, immediately, with both
~~our~~ your and our advantage.

      Entirely yours,
      K. Tanabe.

  "*to our mutual advantage*" you mean;
  but you cannot say that in a
    business = letter.

書店に本を注文すること
明治23年12月11日　松江

_____様

「手紙を書く人のために」といった書物は昨今非常に沢山ありますが、私たちクラス全員が持ちたいと願うような完璧な本がまだほとんど無いのが不満です。もし、貴店に私たちが満足のいくいい本があれば、是非早速一冊値段を添えてお送り下さい。それは貴店と私、両方に好都合となります。

      敬具
      田辺 K.

「お互いの利益のために(*to our mutual advantage*)」ということか、しかし、この表現は商用の手紙では使えません。

【39】To My Father 父へ

To My Father.   5th year.

Matsue, March, 24th
29th Meiji.

My dear father,

This month being about ended, my money, which I received from you only about thirty days ago, is all gone, while I have still you more to pay. I am sorry to have incurred expenses above the amount of my allowance; but none of the money was wasted, and you know well your son is not a spendthrift, but I had many accidental expenses which were unavoidable. Please, send me some sum as soon as possible. Though the spring is fine, it is still cold; I hope you will take good care not to catch cold.   Your dearest son
                K. Tanabe.

To My Father.   5th year.

    Matsuye, March, 24th
            23d Meiji.

My dear father,
              being
~~having~~ t<T>his month ∧ about
                      i
ended, my money, which I receṽed
from you only about thirty days ago,
is all gone, while I have still 3
            I am sorry to have
yen more to pay. ~~This is never very~~
incurred expenses above the amount of my allowance;
~~much pass the proper bounds~~ ; but <none>
   of the money was
~~it is never~~ ∧ waste<d>, and you know
                     a spendthrift.
well your son is not ~~waster~~ ∧ ; but
I had many accidental expenses
which were ~~not~~ <un>avoidable. Please,
send me some sum as soon as
possible.   Though the spring
is fine, it is still cold; I hope you
will
~~shall~~ take a̸ good care not to
catch
~~caught~~ cold.   Your dearest son,
                  K. Tanabe.

親愛なるお父さん、

　今月も終わりを迎えていますが、ほんの30日ほど前に送っていただいたお金は全て使い果たしました。でも、私はまだ3円分支払わなければならないものがあります。限られた小遣いの額を越えてしまって申し訳ありません、しかし無駄使いは一銭もしておりません。あなたの息子であるこの私が浪費家ではないことはご存じの通りです。避けられない多くの予期しない出費がありました。できる限り早くお金を送ってください。春は天気はいいのですがまだまだ寒いです。風邪をひかないように気をつけてください。

　　　　　　　　　最愛の息子
　　　　　　　　　田辺 K.

【40】Tea 茶

Tea.

5th year. K. Tanabe

Tea is ~~the~~ the chief ~~~~ ~~important~~ product of Japan, China, and some other eastern countries. It is the dried leaves of a Chinese shrub, or tea-tree; and there are two species of it in Japan, which we call "sencha" and "bancha", the former being made of tender leaves, and the latter, of old leaves. Wherever we go through our country, tea-trees are cultivated especially ~~at~~ "along" (or "on") the banks of the River Uji in Yamashiro, ~~being~~ which is the most famous and ~~venerable place for tea-culture~~ in Japan. It is our general custom to take the ~~liquor~~ decoction made of it, after meals or when we are very thirsty, instead of taking hot water, because the former is more
(1) ~~tasteful~~ agreeable than the latter; and if we drink it ~~whenever~~ when we are sleepy, we

"Tasteful" is an artistic word only. We say "tasteful dress", "tasteful decoration", "tasteful display of flowers". But we cannot say "tasteful food" or "tasteful drink".

Tea.

    5th year. K.Tanabe.

 Tea is ~~the~~ *the* chief ~~and important~~ product of Japan, China, and some other eastern countries. It is the dried leaves of *a* Chinese shrub or tea-tree; and there are two species of it in Japan, which we call "sencha" and "bancha", the former being made of tender leaves, and the latter, of old leaves. Wherever we go through our country, tea trees are cultivated especially ~~at~~ *"along" (or "on")* the banks of the River Uji in Yamashiro, ~~being~~ *which is* the most famous and ~~noticeable~~ *remarkable place for tea-culture* in Japan. It is our general custom to take the *decoction* ~~liquor~~ made of it, after meal<s>, or when we are very thirst<y>, instead of taking hot water, because the former is more (1) ~~tasteful~~ *agreeable* than the latter; and if we drink it when~~ever~~ we are sleepy, we

 "Tasteful" is an <u>artistic</u> word <u>only</u>. We say "tasteful dress," "tasteful decoration," "tasteful display of flowers." But we <u>cannot</u> say "tasteful food" or "tasteful drink."

茶

  5年 田辺 K.

お茶は日本や中国やその他の東洋の国々では主要な産物です。それは、中国茶の低木から摘まれた葉を乾燥させたものです。また、日本には２種類のお茶があり、私たちはそれを煎茶と番茶と呼んでいます。前者は早摘み、後者は遅摘みとなっています。私たちの国ならどこへ行っても、お茶の木が栽培されています。特に、山城の宇治川の土手沿いは、日本で最もきわだって有名なお茶の産地です。食事の後や喉がとても渇いた時にはお湯を飲む代わりに、お茶でできた煎じ薬を飲むのが私たちの一般的な習慣です。なぜなら煎茶は番茶よりも好みに合うのです。私たちが眠たい時にお茶を飲むと

 "Tasteful"は<u>芸術的な</u>言葉として<u>だけ</u>使われる。英語では「tasteful dress(趣のあるドレス)」「tasteful decoration(趣のある装飾)」「tasteful display of flowers(趣のある花の展示)」とは言いますが、「tasteful food(趣のある食べ物)」「tasteful drink(趣のある飲み物)」とは<u>言えない</u>。

[40] Tea 茶 173

soon become wakeful. But we must take care not to take it too much of it, for it will spoil our stomach.

~~shall~~ soon become wake<*ful*>. But we must
take ~~a~~ care not to take ~~it~~ too
     of it
much ∧ ; for it will spoil our stomach.

すぐに眠れなくなってしまいます。しかし、私たちはお茶をあまり多く飲み過ぎないように気をつけなければなりません。でないとお腹をこわすことになるのです。

【41】The Owl　梟

The Owl.

6th class, K. Tanabe.

The owl is a large raptorial bird, like the kite, belonging to the Nocturnal, while the latter belongs to the Diurnal birds of prey. It dislikes very much to meet with sunshine, it hides always in the hollow of a tree in a deep forest during the day, and in the evening it leaves its shelter and seeks for food, or small birds, wild mice, frogs and several insects, through the whole night. It utters low always dismal and melancholy cries; its whole body is generally brown; its face has some resemblance to the cat's; it has very large and round eyes, and they are set in front of its head, while any other bird's are set at the sides; it has a very sharp bill crooked at the

The Owl.

    5<u>th</u> class, K. Tanabe.

The owl is a large raptorial bird, ~~as~~ *like* the kite, belonging to the Nocturnal, while the latter belongs ^*to* /// the *birds of prey.* Diurnal As it dislikes very much to meets with sunshine, it hides always in ~~a cave of~~ *the hollow of a* tree in a deep forest during the day, and in the evening it leaves the shelter ~~and seeks the~~ *for* food, or small birds, wild ~~mouse~~ *mice*, frogs and several insects, through the whole night. It ~~gives~~ always ^ ~~small~~ *utters low* and *dismal* melancholy cries; its whole body is generally brown; its face ~~shares the~~ *has some* resem~~bre~~blance ~~with~~ *to* the cat's; it has very large and round eyes, and they ~~look toward the front~~ ^ *are set in front of its head* while ~~any~~ *every* other bird's ~~look~~ ^ *are set at* the sides; it has ^ *a* very sharp bill crooked at the

梟

   5組　田辺 K.

梟は、鳶（トビ）と同様に大型の猛禽類の鳥で、夜行性に属します。一方で鳶は昼行性に属します。陽の光をきらうために、日中はいつも深い森の中で、木の窪みに隠れている。そして日が暮れると、隠れ家を出て、小さな鳥、野生のネズミ、蛙や昆虫といった餌を夜通しで探しにいきます。梟はいつも低く不気味な鳴き声を出し、その体軀は一般によく知られている。顔は猫に似ており、大きくて丸い目は顔の前面にあり、他の鳥の目が顔の側面に位置しているのとは異なっています。嘴はとても鋭く、先の方では湾曲しています。

~~foot~~ End; and it is all covered with soft feathers from the head to the tip of the toes, each of which is armed with a very acute nail.

end end; and it is all covered with soft feathers from the head to the tip of the toes, each of which is armed with a very aecute nail.

さらに、梟は頭のてっぺんから脚の先まで柔らかな毛で覆われており、つま先の先端には鋭くとがった爪があります。

About what I Dislike.

5th. year, K. Tanabe.

I do not like an idler, a drunkard, a spendthrift, and a liar, very much, and a liar is especially to be avoided. There is a very respectable and a very important saying:— "one who tells a lie is learning to steal really, and, at last he will be a great thief." No one does not mean of course to be a thief at first, but beginning little and little, and if we tell a single lie we must invent very many others to maintain that one. It is, therefore, sure that Ishikawa Goemon, the very greatest thief who ever lived in Japan, must have been a very little liar at first, and also that lying is bred by idleness, drinking and spending.

About what I Dislike.
　　　　　5th year, K.Tanabe.

I do not like an idler, a drunkard,
　　　　　　or
a spendthrift, ~~and~~ ∧ a liar, very much,
　　　　　　　　　to be avoided.
and a liar is especially ~~avoidable~~.
There is a very respectable and a very important saying: ― "one who tells a lie is learning to steal really, and at last he
　will
~~shall~~ ∧ be a great thief." No one does not mean of course to be a thief at first,
　　　ning
but begins ∧ by little and little, and if we tell a single lie we must invent very many others to maintain that one. It is, therefore, sure that Ishikawa Goemon, the very great<*est*> thief who ~~had~~ ever lived in
　　　　　　　　　　very
Japan, must had<*ve*> been a ∧ little liar at first,
　　　　　　　　lying
and also that ~~a little liar~~ is bred by ~~an~~ idleness, ~~a~~ drinking and ~~a~~ spending.

私の嫌いなものについて
　　　　　5年　田辺 K.

私は怠け者、大酒飲み、金遣いの荒い者、そして嘘つきが大嫌いである。とりわけ、嘘つきにはなりたくない。れっきとした、大変大切な諺―「嘘つきは泥棒の始まり」があります。もちろん、始めから誰も泥棒になろうとは考えていません。しかし少しずつ嘘をつき始め、そして、一つ嘘をつくと、その嘘に辻褄を合わせるためにさらに多くの他の嘘をつかなくてはならなくなります。日本には石川五右衛門というとてつもない大泥棒が確かに実在していましたが、彼は最初はとても小さな嘘つきだったにちがいありません。それにしても嘘は怠惰、飲酒、浪費によってどんどん増長されるものなのです。

[43] The Kite 鳶

The Kite.

1st class, K. Tanabe.

The Kite is a large raptorial bird which belongs to the Falconidae among the diurnal raptores. As it may be seen easily everywhere, we have often an opportunity for observation of its appearance and instincts. — its nature is very valiant; it whole body is brown; its eyes are very large and sharp, being somewhat sunken; its bill is exceedingly acute, hooked at the end; its talons, by means of which it may get its food, or some small animals and rotten meats, are very strong; and that it has eyebrows is a particularity of this family.

The Kite.
   5th Class, K. Tanabe.

The kite is a large raptorial bird
which belongs to the Falconidae among
the Diurnal raptores. As it may
be seen easily everywhere, we have
often an opportunity for observations
of its appearance and instincts: −
its nature is very valiant; its whole
body is brown; its eyes are very
large and sharp, being somewhat sunken; its bill is exceedingly acute,
    -ed
hook~~ing~~ at the end; its talo<*ns*>, by
~~the~~ means of which it may get ~~the~~ *its*
food, or some small animals and
rotten meat~~s~~ , are very strong; and
       a
that it has ~~the~~ eyebrows is ∧ ~~the~~ parti-
cular<*ity*> of this family.

鳶
  5組　田辺 K.

鳶は大型の肉食鳥類で、昼行性猛禽類のハヤブサ科に属している。鳶はどこででも容易に遭遇することができ、鳶の外見や本能を観察する機会にはこと欠かない。鳶は元来とても勇敢で、体全体は茶色である。目は大きくて鋭く、幾分か窪んでいる。嘴は、先まで非常に鋭く、嘴の先端は湾曲している。足首は、小動物や餌の肉をつかむ力がとても強い。さらに種としての鳶は眉をもつという特徴がある。

【44】The lotus 蓮

The lotus.
　　　5th class. K. Tanabe.

　The lotus is a little plant blooming in the summer, in marshes or swamps.[1] Its flower, in spite of sprout (growing) in the mud, is very fine and beautiful; therefore, there is a saying belonging (about) to a great man who extricates himself freely (easily) from every temptation:— "He is like a lotus flower glowing in the mud". And it is regarded with respect by Buddhists, in Japan, as the sacred flower; because they believed that, they may sit down at ease on that flower at the day of judgment, if they made do right through (in) this world.

[1] A "marsh" and a "swamp" is nearly the same thing.
[2] "sprout" is a word referring to the first young growth of a plant — not of the flower.
[3] "Extricate" mean "to free"

The lotus.
            5Th class, K. Tanabe.

The lotus is a little plant blooming in the summer, in marshes or swamps.(1) Its flower, in spite of ~~sprout~~ ^*(2)growing* in the mud, is very fine and beautiful; therefore, there is a say‐ing ~~belonging to~~ *about* a great man who extricates(3) himself ~~freely~~ *easily* from every temptation: ‐ "He is like a lotus flower glowing in the mud". And it is regarded with respect by ~~a~~ Buddhist<s>, in Japan, as the sacred flower; because they believed that, they may sit down at ease on that flower at the day of judgment, if they ~~made~~ *do* right ~~through~~ *in* this world.

(1) A "marsh" and a "swamp" is nearly the same thing.
(2) "Sprout" is a word referring to the first young growth of a <u>plant</u> ‐ not of the <u>flower</u>.
(3) "Extricate" means "to free"

蓮
            5組, 田辺 K.

蓮は小さな植物で、夏に湿地や沼地などで花を咲かせる。泥の中で芽を出すにもかかわらず蓮の花は非常にきれいで美しい。それゆえあらゆる誘惑から己を解き放った佳人について言うときの「彼は泥中に咲く蓮の如し」という俚諺がある。その理由は、日本においては、蓮は神聖な花として仏教徒によって尊ばれている。という事情がある。仏教では、現世において正しい行いをすれば、審判の日には蓮の花の上に腰を下ろし安らぎをえることができると信じられているからである。

(1) "marsh"と"swamp"は、ほとんど同じものです。
(2) "sprout"という言葉は、最初に発芽する植物の若い芽のことをいいます—<u>花</u>の芽ではありません。
(3) "extricate"とは「解き放つ」という意味です。

【45】Lacquer ware 漆器

Lacquer ware.

5th Class, K. Tanabe.

The art of lacquering is a fine art which the Japanese alone possessed from ancient times; our house furniture[1], for the most part, are lacquerware, of which the common ones are cups, dishes, saucers, desks, bureaus, wooden clogs, &c.

This art was developed greatly from the reign of an Emperor Monmu, about 1,200 years ago, and the more generations passed the more the art advanced. At the present day it has made great progress, and attained to perfect skill, being one of the most valuable products, and of the most excellent exports.

(1) The word "furniture" is itself plural, — so that you cannot write "furnitures."

Lacquer w<*a*>re.

5th class, K. Tanabe.

The ∧ lacquering is ~~the~~ ∧ fine art which ~~belonged to~~ the Japanese ~~only~~ ∧ from ancient times; our ∧ house furnitures⁽¹⁾ ~~, for the most part, therefore, on the whole,~~ are lacquer ware, of which the common ones are cups, dishs, saucers, chests, bureaus, wooden-clogs, or etc.
(above insertions: *art of*, *a*, *alone possessed*, *articles of*)

This art was developed greatly from the reign of an Emperor Monmu, about 1,200 years ago, and the more generations passed the more the art advanced.   Thus at the present day it has made great progress, and attained to perfect skill, being one of the most valuable products, and of the most excellent exports.

(1) *The word "furniture" is itself plural, ― so that you cannot write "furnitures."*

漆器

5組　田辺 K.

漆塗りの技術はすばらしく、日本人だけが古代からもち続けてきた技である。私たちの家具⁽¹⁾の大部分は、漆器である。一般的によく見るものは盃、食器類、受け皿、箱類、机、下駄などである。

この漆塗りの技術は、文武天皇の頃から発展し、今から1200年も昔にさかのぼる。そして、時代が移るごとにこの技は進化した。こうして現在では、漆器は偉大な進歩を遂げ、完璧なる技術をもって最高の価値のある産物の一つとなり、もっとも優れた輸出品にもなっている。

（1）"furniture"という単語は、それ自体で複数形である。―それで、"furnitures"と書くことはできません。

[46] Fire-men 消防士

Fire-men.

5th Class. K. Tanabe.

Whose working, at the time of a fire, is the most useful and valuable? I do not need to say that it is that of the fire-men. They work bravely and daringly, in the midst of flames and smoke, taking little care for themselves; and preserve many important buildings which are wrapped in blazing fire, and save many lives of persons and have been cut off from any escape and would otherwise be compelled to perish in flames. Some years ago, a terrible fire broke out in the city of Tokyo, and many lives and buildings were lost; but it was much less hurt than it would otherwise have been, through the efforts of the fire-men. Fire-men are very useful, indeed.

Fire-men.

5th Class. K. Tanabe.

~~What is one~~ <W>hose working, at the
time of a fire, is ∧ *the* most useful and
valuable? I do not need to say
that it is ∧ *that of the* firemen. They work bravely
and daringly, in the ~~middle~~ middst
of flames and smoke, taking little
care for themselves; and ∧ *they* preserve many
important buildings which are wrapped
in blazing fire, and save many lives
of persons who have been
~~which are~~ cut off from any escape
would otherwise be
and ~~are~~ compelled to perish in flames.
Some years ago, a terrible fire broke
out in the city of Tokyo, and many
lives and buildings were lost, but
it was much less hurt than it
through
would otherwise have been, ~~by~~ the
efforts of the
~~means of~~ fire-men. ~~Thus,~~ <F>iremen
are very useful, indeed.

消防士

5組　田辺K.

火事が起きたとき、一体誰の働きが一番役に立ち、価値あるものとなるのだろうか？言うまでもなくそれは消防士である。彼らは、炎と煙の真っ只中で自分たちの危険をかえりみず、勇敢かつ恐れることなく仕事を完遂する。炎に包まれた家屋の中で、通路を確保したり、逃げ道を閉ざされたために炎の中で死を待つしかない人々の命を救ったりする。数年前のこと、東京の街中で恐ろしい火事が起こった。そして、多くの命と家屋が失われた。しかしながら、消防士のおかげで被害を軽減することができた。消防士は本当に私たちの役に立っています。

【47】The Uguisu—(The name of a Japanese Singing-bird)　鶯—（日本の歌鳥の名前）

The Uguisu—(The name of a Japanese Singing-bird.)

5th, K. Tanabe.

There are very many kinds of Singing-birds in Japan, but I prefer the uguisu, (or, as we should call it in English, the nightingale, though it is not exactly the same,) to its others. It is most ~~dexterous~~ accomplished [1] singer which comes early ~~at the~~ in Spring and keeps up its singing to the beginning of the Summer. If we ~~took~~ take a walk in a field, which is covered with many fragrant flowers, in the Spring, we will see many small birds,— uguisu, which are scarcely attractive in ~~their~~ appearances, but the notes ~~tunes~~ of which, mingling with the gentle murmurs of the tender leaves stirred by the breeze, are so enticing and sweet ~~consoling~~ that even the rustics can ~~could~~ not hear them with indifference.

(1) "Dexterous" refers to skillful use of the limbs only,—especially of the hands. "Dexterous" really has the signification of "right-handedness," or one who uses the right hand (dexter) well.

The Uguisu – (The name of a Japanese Singing-bird.)
5th. K. Tanabe.

There are very many kinds of singing-birds in Japan, but I prefer ^*the* uguisu, (or, as we should call it in English, ^*the* nightingale, though ^*it is* not exactly ^*the* same,) to the others. It is most[(1)] ~~dexterous~~ *accomplished* singer which comes early ~~at the~~ ^*in* spring and keeps up its singing to the beginning of the summer.

If we ~~took~~ ^*take* a walk in a field, which is covered with many fragrant flowers, in the spring, we will see many small birds, – uguisu, which are scarcely attractive in ~~the~~ appearances, but the ~~tunes~~ *notes* of which, mingling with the gentle murmurs of ^*the* tender leaves stirred by the ~~sweet~~ breeze, are so entic~~eable~~ *ing* and ##### that even the rustics ~~could~~ ^*can* not hear <them> with indifference.

(1) "Dexterous" refers to skillful use of the limbs only, – especially of the hands. "Dexterous" really has the signification of "right-handedness," or one who uses the right hand (dexter) well.

鶯－（日本の歌鳥の名前）
5年　田辺　K.

日本には、多種の歌鳥がいるが、私は他のどの鳥よりも鶯が好きである。（英語では「ナイチンゲール」と呼ばれているが正確には同じ鳥ではない。）鶯は、実に上手な歌い手で、春先にやって来ては初夏の頃まで歌いつづける。春に、花の香りがいっぱいの原野を歩けばたくさんの小鳥たちに出会う。鶯は、外見こそ見映えはしないが、その鳴き声は、そよ風にゆらぐ柔らかな葉音の穏やかさと調和して魅惑的でとても美しい。田舎に住んでいる人でさえ、その声に無関心ではおられない。

(1) "dexterous"はもっぱら<u>手足</u>の器用さ、特に手の器用さを意味します。"<u>dexterous</u>"には実際には「<u>右利き</u>」つまり右手を上手く使う人という意味があります。

【48】Composition:[Emperor]　作文：[天皇]

Composition

5th　K. Tanabe.

There is one and only one Empire in the world which has always been ruled by only one line of Emperors, unbroken throughout all ages — Japan. The Emperor of Japan is indeed sacred and worthy of all reverence. We mention Him by the names of Heika or Shujō, either of which means His Majesty. He governs the empire very benevolently, and desires to promote the welfare of all, and to give development to the intellectual faculties of his subjects. We must, therefore, serve Him reverently and patriotically, and must be ready to sacrifice our lives for Him and our country, and it is our proper duty to pay several taxes, to serve in the Army or Navy, and besides, by all means, to work to improve the prosperity of the Empire.

— "Eternal" means "that which has no beginning and no end."

Composition

          5<u>th</u> K. Tanabe.

There is one and only one Empire in the world which is ~~reigned by~~ *has always been ruled by only* ∧ one line of Emperors, unbroken ~~for eternal~~ *throughout all* ages —— Japan. The Emperor of Japan is indeed sacred and ~~inviolable~~ *worthy of all reverence*. We mention Him by ∧*the* names of ~~the~~ Heika or Shujō, either of which means His Majesty. He governs the empire very benevolently, and desires to ~~b~~ promote the welfare of ∧*all*, and to give ~~def~~ development to the intellectual faculty<*ies*> of ~~its~~ ∧*his* subjects. We must, therefore, serve Him reverently and patriotically, and must be ready to sacrifice our ~~life~~ ∧*lives* for Him and ~~his~~ ∧*our* country, and it is our proper ~~dity~~ duty to pay several taxes, to serve ∧*in* the Army or Navy, and besides, by all measures, to work to improve the ~~pros~~ prosperity of the Empire.

―――――

-"Eternal" means "that which has no beginning and no end."

[49] Swimming 水泳

Swimming.
                5th year, K. Tanabe.

In midsummer, the weather is exceeding hot, the thermometer rises very high, the earth is greatly scorched, plants are almost withered, and our bodies become intensely heated, our energy gradually decreases; at last we feel a head-ache, and then we are compelled to abandon our tasks, to gape, and to take a nap. On these days one, and only one exercise can revive us from such prostration, is the art of moving through the water by means of the limbs, that is to say, swimming. In fact, swimming, in these days, is the most interesting and delightful method, except when practised to excess, of rendering our bodies cool and healthy, and of keeping our minds so fresh and merry that we feel as if revived. Moreover, there is a more important

Swimming.

5th year, K. Tanabe.

In middle summer, ⟨the⟩ weather is exceedingly hot, ⟨the⟩ thermometer ~~points out~~ ⟨rises⟩ very high ~~power~~, ⟨the⟩ earth is greatly schorched, plants are almost wither<ed>, and our bod<ies> become intense<ly> heat<ed>, our energy gradually decrease<s>;— at last we feel a head-ache and then we are compelled to ~~give up our mind to~~ ⟨abandon⟩ our task<s> to gape, and to take a nap ~~only~~. ⟨On⟩ ~~At~~ these days one, and only one ~~proeges~~ ⟨exercise⟩ ~~process~~, which ~~restore~~ ⟨can revive⟩ us from such prostration, ~~disasters~~, is the art of moving ~~on~~ ⟨through the⟩ water by means of the limbs, — that is ⟨to say,⟩ swimming. In fact, swimming, in these days, is the most interesting and delightful method, ~~except excessive~~ ⟨except when practised to excess⟩, of rendering our bod<ies> cool and healthy, and of ~~inducing~~ ⟨keeping⟩ our minds so ~~pure~~ ⟨fresh⟩ and merry that we feel as if ~~we~~ revived. Moreover, there is ~~the~~ ⟨a⟩ more important use of swimming. If we find ourselves in deep water, through shipwreck, or from any other cause, we can save ourselves easily by the means of this art, while, if we are ignorant of it we may lose our lives*. Here is an account which I have learned from my teacher:— in the British island, there was a boy named Mark Fay, large & strong but idle. It was his usual habit to answer "O! what is the use?" whenever he was urged to study. Once when he was urged by a friend to learn to swim, he answered the same word, and of course he did not learn. After some days his sister Jane fell into the brook, from the bridge that was near their school; at the time he was in consternation only, not knowing how to do, so he stared and cried. But the poor girl was saved by an other small boy, John Bruce, who was younger and smaller than Mark, and Mark

* "Rescue" is only used of saving others, not of saving ourselves.

use o‹for› swimming, too.　If we ~~drowned~~
find ourselves in deep water
~~in water by wreck~~ ∧or∧ any other cause,
through shipwreck from
we ~~will rescue~~* ourselves easily by the
can save
means of ~~art~~ this art, while, if we ∧ ignorant,
are
~~we could have die~~.　Here is an ac-
of it we may lose our lives
count which I have learned from
my teachers: —— in the British island,
there ~~is~~ ∧ a boy named Mark Fay, large &
was
strong but idle.　It was his usual habit
to answer! "O! what is the use?" whenever he
was urged to study. Once when he was urged
by a friend to learn to swim, he answered
the same word, and of course he did
not learn. After some days his sister
Jane fell in‹to› the brook, ∧ the bridge that
from
was near their school; at the time he
was in consternation only, not knowing
how to do, so he stared and cried.
But the poor girl was saved by ~~the~~ ∧ other
an
small boy, John Brande, who was younger
and smaller than Mark, and Mark

―――
* "Rescue" is only used of saving others,
  – not of saving ourselves.

もし、私たちが船の難破や他の何らかの原因で水の深みに溺れたなら私たちはこの泳ぎの技術を知っていることによって助かる*のだ。他方、もし泳ぎを知らないなら生命を失うことになるだろう。ここに私が先生たちから教わった話がある：——英国にマーク・フエイという名前の体格が大きく頑丈ではあるが怠惰な少年がいた。彼は何かを学ぶように言われるといつも「何の役に立つの？」と答えるのが癖だった。ある時、彼が友達から泳ぎ方を習うように言われた時、彼は同じ言い方で答えた。そして彼はもちろん学ぼうとはしなかった。何日かして彼の妹のジェーンが学校の近くにある橋から落ちた時、どうしていいかわからずただうろたえて叫びながら見ていただけであった。しかし、可哀想なその少女は別の小さなジョン・ブランドという男の子に助けられた。彼はマークよりも年下で体も小さかった。そこでマークは

―――
* 「Rescue」は、他人を助ける時にのみ使われる言葉で、―自分を助ける時には使わない。

then ~~was blushed~~ ashamed and mute. — This account gives us a very important lesson, that swimming is ~~the requisite and is~~ an indispensable accomplishment.

Good.

    ashamed
then was ~~blushed~~ and mute. – This
account gives us a very important lesson, that swimming is ~~the requisite and~~
   an
~~the~~ ∧ indispensable accomplishment.

   Good.

その時、恥ずかしくなり言葉を失っていた。—この話はひとつの大切な教訓として水泳は欠くことのできない身についた技能であることを私たちに教えてくれている。

  よろしい

【50】 To answer the question, "What are you going to do after you have finished your studies in the Chiugakkō?"

「中学校を卒業して貴方はどうするのか？」という問いに答えて

To answer the question, "What are you going to do after you have finished your studies in the Chiugakkō?"

5th. H. Tanabe.

I have often been asked by my parent and brothers about this very question, and whenever they asked I replied "please, give me a little more time to think about it." Indeed, this is too important a fact to be determined heedlessly, and is too serious a question to be answered inconsiderately, because if I should make a mistake in choosing a profession, it is certain that I would suffer many misfortunes. Therefore I have not yet fully made up my mind what career I will adopt; but for the present, my hope is to become a physician.

Very good indeed! Do not be discouraged by your few mistakes. I think you will write English very nicely some day. Read all the interesting English books you can get.

100

To Answer the question, "What are you going to do after you have finished your studies in the Chiugakkô?"

5th. K. Tanabe.

I have ^*often* been ~~always~~ asked by ~~the~~ *my* parents and brothers about this very question, and whenever they asked I replied " please, give me a little more time to think about it." In *very* <*In*>deed, this is too important a fact to ^*be* determined heedlessly, and is too serious ^*a* question to ^*be* answered inconsiderately, because if I should *make a mistake in choosing a profession* ~~mistook to choose a course~~, it is certain that I ~~am to fall into a great calamities~~ *would suffer many great misfortunes*. Therefore I ~~do not yet determine firmly~~ *have not yet fully made up my mind* what ~~a course I take~~ *career I will adopt*; but for the ~~most part~~ *present*, my hope is to become a physician.

> Very good indeed! Do not be discouraged by your few mistakes. I think you will write English very nicely some day. Read all the interesting English books you can get.
>
> 100

「中学校を卒業して貴方はどうするのか？」という問いに答えて。

5年　田辺　K.

この問いはよく親や兄弟たちから聞かされてきました。また、他人がこの問いを発する時にはいつも私は「もう少し考える時間をください」と答えてきました。実際、このことはあまりにも重要なことなので不用意には決められないことなのです。これはまたとても厳粛な問題なので軽率に答えることはできませんでした。もし私が職業選択を間違えたら、間違いなく多くの不運に遭遇することになります。またそれ故、私は自分がどんな仕事に就くかはまだ決めるに至っていません。しかし現時点では私の希望は医者になることです。

とてもよくできました！少しくらいの間違いにくじけないこと。あなたはそのうち英語をとても上手く書けるようになると思います。手に入る興味深い英語の本を全て読んでみなさい。

100

ハーンによる英作文添削の分類と分析

はじめに

　ラフカディオ・ハーン（小泉八雲）は一方で夢想豊かな作家であり、他方で事象の報告・執筆をよくこなす有能なジャーナリストであったが、加えて教壇に立つ人間としてすぐれた教育者でもあった。ジャーナリストは自らの目と耳で取材したものを文字を使って伝えるというスタンスをもつ。ハーンはこのスタンスを保ちながらも、同時に日本の教育現場に関ってこれを直接〈取材〉し、ここから得たものを英語という西洋の言語でリポートするのである。ハーン作品のうち、松江での"From the Diary of an English Teacher"（「ある英語教師の日記から」）、熊本での"With Kyushu Students"（「九州の学生とともに」）はその代表的なものである。

　立場の弱い者、周縁部にいる者、差別されている者などに共感する心をもっていたハーンは教育者としても優れた資質を備えていた。シンシナティ時代は公立図書館に通いつめてさまざまな領域の書物を独学で学び、フランス文学の英語への翻訳もこの頃から手がけている。ニューオーリンズではクレオール文化と接触し、土地のクレオール料理の本を著し、カリブ海周辺の六つの地域からの俚諺を整理し、これにクレオール語、フランス語、英語の三層の説明を加えた Gombo Zhèbes（『ゴンボ・ゼーブ』）という瀟洒な小辞典を作成している。

　ハーパーズ・マガジン社からの特派員として来日する前にハーンはすでにバジル・ホール・チェンバレンの『古事記』の英訳本を読んでいた。来日後もハーンは自ら学んだ日本のこと、特に神道や仏教の知識も豊かになり、優れた記憶力とものごとを分かりやすく説明する能力をもって良き教師として生徒たちに慕われていた。

　教育とは元来「教え育てる」ことである。また英語の educate の語源は人の潜在能力を「引き出すこと」である。ハーンは高学歴や教員の免許状のようなものはなかったが、学生たちに対する〈共感〉の能力をよくもっていた。そして西洋人でありながら日本人の心を深く理解しようとし、この心は生徒たちにも十分に伝わり、彼らもこのようなハーンの心によく応えたのであった。

　ハーンが特派員の延長線上にあって日本で島根県尋常中学校、熊本の第五高等中学校、東京帝国大学、早稲田大学と教育者として生活の舞台で「教える」という視点が大きく関わってくるわけであるが、ここには次のようなユニークな特徴があった。(i) 学歴、資格などに関らず外国人教師として生徒と同じ目線で関ることができた。(ii) 外国人であるがゆえにハーンは日本の日常的な事象をどこまでも対象化しながら観察、記述することができた。(iii) 体系的ではないが体験的、実証的な日本についての記述あるいは記録に専念することができ、内容は恒に具体的であった。

　田部隆次の『小泉八雲』の第七章「横浜から松江」の章には、ハーンは暇さえあれば松江市中をあさって骨董や浮世絵を買い、市中や近郊の神社仏閣名所旧跡を訪ねたことに加えて、尋常中学の生徒には「牡丹」「狐」「蚊」「幽霊」「亀」「蛍」「ホトトギス」の如き題を与えて英作文を作らせ孜々として日本研究を怠らなかった、とある。生徒にとっては英作文の授業ではあるが、ハーンにとっては格好の日本理解のための資料であったというわけである。このことを裏付ける基礎資料がかなりの量出てきたのである。これらはハーンが来日後松江で教鞭を取っていたころのもので、英作文の授業でハーンが出題し、添削して学生に返却したものがガラス乾板というか

たちで熊本県立図書館に保管されていたものである。

このガラス乾板は元々熊本にゆかりの深い劇作家木下順二氏が小泉八雲熊本旧居に送り、これが県立図書館に渡ったものである。そしてこれはハーンの松江時代の教え子である大谷正信と田辺勝太郎のものであった。しかしこのガラス乾板のもとになる原物の所在は一部を除いて今も分からない。どこか行方不明のままか、先の大戦で焼失してしまっている可能性が高い。その一部とは京都外国語大学に断片的に十数枚原物が保管されているが、これと比較してもこの新たに見つかったガラス乾板の量は多い。

ハーンは教師として授業の英作文の添削や授業スタイルには生徒たちに共感の姿勢を強くもっていた。西野影四郎（2000）はハーンが生徒からSirと呼ばれるのを嫌がり、「教師と生徒は兄弟の関係だった」と言っていたことについて触れている。また英語の加筆修正の部分についてはその内容にかなり詳しいコメントが書き込まれているのである。本稿ではこのような経緯をもったガラス乾板に残されている二人の生徒のハーンによる英作文添削の内容の紹介と分類・分析を行いたいと思う。

生徒の英作文添削にみるハーン

ハーンは1890年（明治23年）8月30日（土）に松江に入り冨田屋旅館に投宿。ここで教頭であった西田千太郎と会い互いに心を通わせる。そして9月3日(水)から授業を始めている。前任者はカナダ人教師タットル氏であった。ハーンは形式主義、序列主義を嫌った。タットル氏は西洋人特有の宣教的態度の持ち主で授業もリーディングが中心であった。これに対してハーンは発音や書き取り、英作文など語学の方面から実践的な指導に苦心を払っていた。ハーンの授業は恒に学生への配慮を欠かさず自らの知識と意見をコメントのなかで生かしていくというスタンスをもっていたのである。

ハーンは『知られぬ日本の面影』の中の「英語教師の日記から」の章において、「日本の生徒を教えることは、かねがね想像していたにもまして、なかなかおもしろいしごとであるあることがわかった。」（平井呈一訳、以下同様）と述べている。〈おもしろい〉というその中身は学生が書く文そのものの内容とスタイルである。そして英語に関しては日本語との大きな違いを乗り越えて学ばねばならぬ点を指摘して「英語は日本語と大いに違っているから、ごく簡単な日本語の句でも、ただ単語の逐語訳や思想の形を直訳しただけでは、英語にわかるように翻訳できないのである」と述べている。

さて、具体的な英作文の添削を行いながら、ハーンは「日本の学生にとって、英語という語学がひじょうにむずかしいことを考えると、わたくしの受け持っている幾人かの生徒の思想の表現力は驚くべきものがある」と言っている。この思想とは当時彼らが受けていた教育の中身であり、それは多少とも当時の明治新政府による国家主義的な教育内容を反映するものであった。

ハーンの英語の授業は松江時代から熊本時代にかけて一貫していた。後に木下順二がかつて実際にハーンの授業を受けた人々から聞いた話として昭和10年4月の五高同窓々報第八号に書いた論考「小泉八雲先生と五高」の中で次のように記している。

「当時の生徒であった方々の御話を伺うと八雲先生の授業の半ばは、生徒の自由作文に費されたようである。何でもいゝから、君達の知って居る日本の昔の話を書いて呉れ、など命じては、生徒に一時間、自由な筆をふるはせられたらしいのである。さうしてその作文は必ず添削して返却された。その添削がまた尋常一様のものでは無い。すみからすみ迄眼を通して、労を

惜まず筆を執られた詳細極まる添削を一人一人の作文に加えて返されたところに、八雲先生の一面が見られる。」

　この論考は木下順二がまだ学生であった五高の二年生の時に書いたものであるがその早熟な才能には驚かされる。
　ハーンはやがて彼らの英作文を添削しながら次のようなことを発見する。「かれらの作文は、たんに個人的な性格のあらわれとしてではなく、国民的な感情、いいかえれば、ある種の綜合的感情のあらわれとして、私にはまた別趣の興味があるのである」。ここでいう国民的感情は日本という国家レベルでの共同体的な伝統主義のなかで育まれていったものである。「日本の学生の英作文を見て、わたくしにもっとも不思議に思われることは、そういう作文に個人的特色というものがまったくない、ということだ。二十篇の英作文の筆跡までが不思議に同族的な似よりをもっているのを発見する。」と看破している。
　ハーンは松江の生徒の中に見出していたものは非西洋的な感性であり、いわば伝統的・集団的な共同幻想の世界であった。ハーンは言う、「日本の学生は想像力という点ではあまり独創性を示さない。かれらの想像力は、もう何百年も前から、一部は中国、一部は日本で、すでにかれらのためにつくられてあるのである」。これは平安時代に遡る伝統的な花鳥風月においても、無常観といった美意識や人生観にも通じている。これは日本人においてはほとんど文化的DNAといってもいいほどの共有と強い伝承・継承の力をもったものなのである。

英作文の出題テーマ
　ハーンは基本的にジャーナリスト魂の染み込んだ心をもって教壇に立っていたが、その際日本人の文化、歴史、風土、宗教などについて理解し、これを西洋に向けてリポートしていた。それが一連のハーン作品となっていたのである。言い換えれば、日本と言う〈東の国から〉西洋という〈西の国に〉向って言葉を発していたのである。媒介となる言語は当然ハーンの母語である英語でなければならなかった。教育現場では個人個人の印象を通して総じて日本人の一般的特徴を抽出しようとしていた。これにはニューオリンズで友人のオスカー・クロスビーを介して紹介された思想家ハーバート・スペンサーの社会進化論的発想が大きな影響を与えている。これは『ラフカディオ・ハーン著作集第四巻』（恒文社）のあとがき・解説の中で千石英世氏が「ハーンは…最も広い意味における人種、つまり個人としての人間を見るのではなく、類として、また種として、すなわち、何らかの集団的特徴へと自身の人間観察を還元していく傾向があるように思われる」と述べていることに通じている。
　種としての人間は生物学的にはともかく文化的・社会的には相対的なものである。文明開化していく日本という国をその心で解釈・理解し、これをニューヨークの『ハーパー』社に取材・報告することをハーンは義務づけられていた。この際来日に際して労を取ってくれた『ハーパーズ・マガジン』社の美術担当記者ウィリアム・パットンとの約束においてハーンは日本理解の契機の一つを教育の現場、特に生徒たちの作り出す英作文内容の中に見い出そうとしたのである。角田羊三（1996）によれば、「作文は自由英作文で、題は松江の名所や生活に直接結びついた題材を除くと生徒の感想を書かせ、文法の誤りを訂正し、いちいち批評を書き添えた」とある。また洗川暢男（1991）も言うように英作文教育においては「自然の観察を重んじているためにできるだけ科学的テーマで自由に作文を書かせる」という面もあったのである。
　見つかったガラス乾板に見られる生徒の名前は大谷正信と田辺勝太郎であるが、ハーンがどの

ような課題（テーマ）を生徒に課していたかについてのリストを以下に記載しておきたい。学年は授業を受けていたときの生徒の学年次またはclass（組）で、作文に名前とともに記載されていたものである。学年の不明なものについては？印をつけておいた。

[大谷正信]
- The Hototogisu　ホトトギス（4年）
- The Greatest Japanese　最も偉大な日本人（4年）
- The greatest Japanese Part II　最も偉大な日本人　そのII（4年）
- The fire-fly　蛍（4年）
- The mountain called Dai-sen　大山と呼ばれる山（4年）
- The Botan　牡丹（4年）
- Hina matsuri　雛祭り（5年）
- What is the most awful thing?　世に最も怖いものは何か？（4年）
- Ghosts　幽霊（？年）
- The Birthday of His Majesty　天皇誕生日（4年）
- Composition：[Creator]　作文：[創造者]（？年）
- Boating on the lake of Shinji　宍道湖をボートで行くこと（4年）
- The Tortoise　亀（4年）
- Lake Shinji　宍道湖（4年）
- About Kasuga at Matsue　松江の春日について（5年）
- The Japanese Monkey　日本猿（4年）
- The fashions of Old Japan Part I – The House　古代日本の様式　そのI－住居（？年）
- The fashions of Old Japan Part II – The Clothing　古代日本の様式　そのII－衣服（4年）
- To Mr. Lafcadio Hearn　ラフカディオ・ハーン先生へ（4年）
- Fencing　剣道（4年）
- About the Gymnastic Contest of Last Saturday　先週土曜日の運動会について（4年）
- The Centipede　百足（4年）
- How did you spend this summer vacation?　この夏休みをどう過ごしましたか？（5年）
- The Owl　梟（4年）
- About the little insects which fly to the lamps at night and burn themselves to death　夜、飛んで灯に入り焼け死ぬ虫について（4年）
- Composition：[An Autumn Walk]　作文：秋の散策（5年）

[田辺勝太郎]
- Rice　米（？年）
- The Seven Deities of Good Fortune　七福神（5年）
- The Frog　蛙（5年）
- The Most wonderful Thing　最も素晴らしいもの（5年）
- Wrestling　相撲（5年）
- Letter about Matsue to a friend　友への松江便り（？学）
- Why should we venerate our Ancestors?　祖先を敬うべき理由は何か？（5年）

- The fox who borrowed the Tiger's Power　虎の威を借る狐（5年）
- The weather of the 15th of January　1月15日の天候（5年）
- The Tortoise　亀（？年）
- The Japanese Spider　日本の蜘蛛（5年）
- To a Bookseller asking for a book　書店に本を注文すること（？年）
- To My Father　父へ（5年）
- Tea　茶（5年）
- The Owl　梟（5年）
- About what I Dislike　私の嫌いなものについて（5年）
- The Kite　鳶（5年）
- The lotus　蓮（5年生）
- Lacquer ware　漆器（5年生）
- Fire-men　消防士（5年生）
- The Uguisu—(The name of a Japanese Singing-bird)　鶯—（日本の歌鳥の名前）（5年）
- Composition：[Emperor]　作文：[天皇]（5年）
- Swimming　水泳（5年）
- To answer the question, "What are you going to do after you have finished your studies in the Chiugakkō?"「中学校を卒業して貴方はどうするのか？」という問いに答えて（5年）

テーマの分類

これを見ると興味深いことが分かる。上記の両者50の課題を概ね以下のように分類することができる。両者に共通してある課題は一つとして数え、同一タイトルでパートⅠとⅡに分かれているものは同一のタイトルと考える。

◇生き物（鳥）：[ホトトギス]　[梟]　[鶯—(日本の歌鳥の名前)]　[鳶]
◇生き物（虫）：[蛍]　[百足]　[日本の蜘蛛]
◇生き物（動物）：「日本猿」　[亀]　[蛙]
◇植物（花）：[牡丹]　[蓮]
◇スポーツ：[剣道]　[相撲]　[水泳]
◇神々と神社：[松江の春日について]　[七福神]　[天皇]
◇霊的なもの：[創造者]　[幽霊]　[祖先を敬うべき理由は何か？]
◇祭日：[雛祭り]　[天皇誕生日]　[先週土曜日の運動会について]
◇伝統的民芸：[漆器]
◇自然風景：[大山と呼ばれる山]　[宍道湖]　[宍道湖をボートで行くこと]
◇趣向：[最も素晴らしいもの]　[私の嫌いなものについて]　[世に最も怖いものは何か？]
　　　　[秋の散策]
◇人事：[消防士]　[最も偉大な日本人]
◇様式（ファッション）：[古代日本の様式：住居]　[古代日本の様式：衣服]
◇生活品：[米]　[茶]
◇実用性：[ラフカディオ・ハーン先生へ]　[書店に本を注文すること]　[父へ]
　　　　　[友への松江便り]

◇ 俚諺：［夜、飛んで灯に入り焼け死ぬ小虫について］　［虎の威を借る狐］
◇ その他：［この夏休みをどう過ごしましたか？］　［1月15日の天候］
　　　　　［「中学校を卒業して貴方はどうするのか？」という問いに答えて］

　これを見るとハーンが松江の学生たちにどのような課題を与えていたかが概ね推測できる。いずれも日本的特徴を色濃く反映したものである。そしてここにはハーン自身の好みも反映されていることが窺える。生き物はすべからく小さい虫で昆虫や爬虫類、両生類、節足動物でどちらかと云えば一般にはグロテスクを感じさせるものである。花は東洋の美意識や仏教的なものを感じさせるものである。スポーツは日本の国技として身近な［剣道］や［相撲］に加えてハーン自身が得意で大好きだった［水泳］が入っているところが興味深い。
　「神々と神社」「霊的なもの」「祭日」の分類では日本精神の根底に流れるアニミズムあるいは日本の古層にある神道的精神風土につながるものが提示されている。「伝統的民芸」を表す品目として［漆器］や祭日の［雛祭り］は身近であり、生活の中で［米］や［茶］の大切さはいうまでもないところである。自然風景としては［大山］や［宍道湖］は日常的な生活の舞台であり、松江の生徒たちを育む原風景であった。これらはおそらくハーンの心の基層にある自然風景と重なるところがあったにちがいない。
　ハーンは、しかし、実生活においては厳格な合理主義者あるいはリアリストであった。子供が将来困らないように実生活上の知恵と知識と能力を幼少時から授けておくという姿勢はつねにハーンの中にあり、彼の子育てのなかでもそれは見られた。興味深いことにこの姿勢が授業の英作文の課題提供という場面でもみられる。たとえば作文を通して生徒が実際に手紙を書く場面を想定して本屋に本を注文するときに書く実用的な手紙や、学費や生活に困ったときに父親にお金を送ってもらう時に書く手紙の書き方などを課題として与えている。そしてどの英作文に対してもそれぞれに丁寧な英語の添削と必要なコメントを与えているのである。

コメントの分析
　資料はハーンが島根県尋常中学校で英語の教師として赴任しているときに生徒に課した英作文に添削を加え、かつ内容についてコメントを加えたものである。彼が教えた生徒たちは当時旧制中学でかなりの知的能力をもっていたと考えられるが、彼の添削コメントは紋切り型ではなく自在さのなかにもハーン自身の考え方が反映されたものですこぶる興味深いものがある。
　コメントの相手が中学生ということで軽くみることはなく、むしろ相手を尊重し、敬意をもって添削にあたっている。その内容は英語の文法的、語法的な面に加えて、語源、文化・文明論、宗教論、聖書の紹介、創造主のこと、生物学的知識など多岐に渡り、内容も中学生にしてはすこぶる高度なものである。折りあるごとにハーンは生徒の英作文の余白にコメントしているが、そのうち次の八つを選んで以下に紹介と分析を試みたい。テーマは「語源」「適者生存の原理」「キリスト教」「神道と仏教」「信仰と礼儀」「創造者」「文明と宗教」「科学」である。ハーンによるコメントの原テキストはイタリック体で示してある。＊の部分は筆者のコメントである。

〈1〉　語源
The generally accepted meaning of Tsuchigumo is "Earth-spider"; and in old Japanese books these cave dwellers are pictured as enormous spiders, — Still, some say, the word is a corruption of Tsuchi-gomori, which would mean "Earth-hiders." Such is the opinion

of the translation of the Ko-ji-ki. 〈一般的に容認された「土蜘蛛」の意味は「土－蜘蛛」であり、古い日本の文献では、これら洞穴居住者は巨大な蜘蛛として描かれている。―さらにこの語彙は「土に隠れるもの」を意味する「土籠り」の訛ったものという人もいる。これは『古事記』の訳者の考え方である。〉

* ハーンは語源の重要さをよく知っていた。すでにニューオリンズの『タイムズ・デモクラット』紙のエセー（1884年11月16日）「頭の中の辞書(Mental Dictionary)」の中から「語の歴史をたずねての語源研究は大いに役立つだろう。いったんその語の歴史を知るとその語は記憶から去ることがけっしてないからである。」を引用している。当時影響力が大きく言語学の世界で意味論を創出したといわれる言語学者ミシェル・ブレアルの言語観を参考にしているのである。中学の生徒の英作文ではあるが、語源への興味を生徒に喚起する意味では特に興味深く大切なコメントであると思われる。

〈2〉 適者生存の原理

Not necessarily. You mean, of course, the doctrine of the "Survival of the fittest," which is no longer only a doctrine, but a positive truth. I have, however, great faith in the force of the Japanese race. 〈必ずしもそうではない。もちろん君は「適者生存」の学説を云っているのだろうが、これはもはや単に学説といったものではなく、もっと積極的な真理というべきものなのだ。それにしても、私は日本民族の力に大きな信頼をおいている。〉

* これは西洋人が無慈悲な文明と経済力に加えてコロニアルな宣教的思想をもって日本に入り、印度や太平洋上の島々のように日本を植民地化してしまうのではないかといった内容に対してハーンがコメントしたものである。ここでハーンは「適者生存」の進化論的原理を引き合いに出している。西洋列強の力は認めつつも日本民族もそれに対応するだけの力があると言っているところが興味深い。ここでH. スペンサーの信奉者としてのハーンを垣間見ることができる。

　　ここで思い出されることは、明治新政府はアジアの一小国を自認しつつ多くのお雇い外国人を招聘し、西洋列強をお手本として日本の近代化・西洋化を目指した。その結果として国力を増強することによってからくも西洋列強から植民地化されることを防いだ。これはハーンから見れば「適者生存」の原理を全うしたことになる。しかしその後日本は東洋における「先進国」としてそれまでアジアでヨーロッパ列強がしたことと同じように植民地政策を行使する国になっていった。

〈3〉 キリスト教

Christianity will never be accepted in Japan, except by vulgar or weakminded people. – I trust. If the Buddhist schools would teach modern science, no Christian missionaries could proselytize the people. Out of 43,000,000 Japanese, the Christians themselves only claim to have about 60,000; and the probable truth is there are not more than 1 and 10 of these Christians in real belief. Here are the texts, you referred to:
　　– "A man shall leave his father and mother, and shall cleave unto his wife"

>   Matthew   19 chap. 5th verse.
> Also – Mark   10   "   7   "
> Also – Genesis   2   "   24   ".

These are the 3 texts of the Bible.
In Europe, a wife does not wish to live with her husband's parents. Once married, the son abandons his parents, – and helps them only in extreme cases. There is not in Europe, any of what is called filial piety in Japan, – except what the hearts of naturally good men make them do. 〈キリスト教は粗野で少し精神の弱い人意外日本では受け入れられないであろう、―と私は信じる。もし仏教諸宗派が近代科学を教えていたとしたら、宣教師は誰一人として人々を改宗させることはできなかっただろう。4300万の日本人のうちクリスチャンは6万人程度と言えるだけだ。そして恐らく当時こうしたクリスチャンのうち10人に1人も本当に信仰をもっていたとは思えない。ここに君が述べていた聖書からの引用がある。―

> 「人はその父と母を離れて、その妻と結ばれる。」（マタイ、19章、5節）、さらに（マルコ、10章、7節）、さらに（創世記、2章、24節）。

これは聖書から取った3つのテキストです。
ヨーロッパでは妻は夫の両親と同居することを望まない。一度結婚したら息子は両親を捨て、余程のことがないと助けることはない。ヨーロッパには日本にあるような<u>慈悲深い哀れみ</u>の心がないのです。――例外的に生まれつき良い心をもった人はそうしますが。〉

*　ここにはコロニアルな宣教的キリスト教を好まないハーンの心情が出ている。聖書の知識は豊かにあることは彼がイギリスのダラム市郊外アショーの聖カスバルト神学校にいたことを考えれば当然のことであるが、彼は生涯の最後まで宗教的あるいは求道的精神態度をもちながらもキリスト教を好意的に書くことはなかった。確かに歴史を通してキリスト教が日本の風土に根付きにくかったことはその通りかもしれない。しかし、ヨーロッパでは子供は結婚したらここで言われているように両親を顧みないというのは恐らく公平さを欠いたコメントであろう。ここでハーンは生徒の文章に対するコメントというかたちを借りて自らの裡にあるキリスト教に対して手厳しい批判を加えている。これはおそらくハーンのトラウマとして少年期に味わった神学校での辛い体験や懐疑心から来るものであろう。

〈4〉　神道と仏教

The Karashishi are of Buddhist origin, although adopted by Shinto, since the time of Ryobu Shinto. 〈唐獅子は両部神道の時代から神道に取り入れられたが、その源は仏教に由来する。〉

*　仏や菩薩がわが国の神祇となって現れたとする本地垂迹説の根底をなす神仏調和の神道が両部神道であるが、ここでハーンは生徒に、唐獅子の由来から仏教に思いを馳せ、それが神道に入ってきたことを説き、日本の思想・宗教史的視点を踏まえて生徒にその由

来を説明しているのである。これはハーン自身のなみなみならぬ日本の神道や仏教への関心と理解のほどが窺える。

〈5〉 信仰と礼儀

Such a man is a hypocrite and an ignoramus. In his own country, he would not dare to enter the room of Her Majesty's Consuls, without taking off his hat. And a Consul is only an humble official of the Queen. 〈このような男は偽善者で無知蒙昧な人間である。自国では帽子も取らずに敢えて女王陛下の執事の部屋に入ることはないだろう。しかも執事は女王陛下に仕えるただの地位の低い役人にしかすぎないのだ。〉

* ここでは原文は「最も怖いもの」というテーマで生徒はクリスチャンと書き、クリスチャンは天皇のご真影に礼をしないと書いている。その個所でハーンはこのコメントを与えているのである。クリスチャンは信仰の問題として偶像崇拝を排する。ハーンはこのことを礼儀の問題と関係させる。イギリスでは執事にすら帽子を取って部屋に入るくらいだから、まして女王には勿論、同じ立場の天皇の写真には礼をすべきだ、としているのである。時代と伝統がそうさせているにしても、クリスチャンたちの信仰の問題と社会規範の礼儀の問題とを考えさせるところにハーンの視点があるように思われる。生徒に少なからぬ影響を与える教育現場にあってハーンのこのコメントは興味深い。

〈6〉 創造主

This argument, (called by Christians Paley's Argument), is absurdly _false_. Because a book is made by a bookmaker, or a watch by a watchmaker, it does not follow at all that Suns and Worlds are made by an intelligent designer. We only know of books and watches as human productions. Even the substance of a book or a watch we do not know the nature of. What we _do_ know logically is that Matter is eternal, and also the Power which shapes it and changes it 〈この考え方は（クリスチャンたちにペイリーの議論と呼ばれているものだが）全くの偽りである。本は本作りによって、時計は時計職人によって作られるからといって、太陽やこの世界が知能の高い一人の設計者によって作られたということにはならない。われわれは本や時計については、それらは人間の作り出した産物であるということが分かっているだけである。われわれには本や時計という物の本質さえ分からないのです。論理的に分かっていることといえば、物質は永遠であり、その物質を形づくり、変える力もまた永遠であるということである。〉

* 本は本作りが、時計は時計職人が創るようにこの世界は一人のすぐれた全知の設計者によって創られたとする考え方がある。これはクリスチャンたちからは「ペイリーの議論」といわれる考え方であるが、これがいかに愚かなものであるかをハーンは指摘する。前者は人間のなせる技であるが、後者はそうではないというのである。この指摘にはハーンの科学的合理主義を尊重する立場が垣間見られる。物質とそれを形作り、形を変える大きな力の存在は永遠のものである、という指摘は彼のなかに科学的真理あるいは創造主の実在への予感を感じさせてくれるものである。

〈7〉 文明と宗教

At one time the Greeks and the Egyptians, both highly civilized people, believed in different gods. Later, the Romans and Greeks, although highly civilized, accepted a foreign belief. Later still, these civilized peoples were conquered by races of a different faith. The religion of Mahomet was at one time that of the highest civilization. At another time, the religion of India was the religion of the highest civilization. It is very doubtful whether the civilization of a people has connection whatever with their religion. — In Christian countries, moreover, the most learned men do not believe in Christianity; and the Christian religion is divided into countless sects, which detest each other. No European scientist of note — no philosopher of high rank — no 'really' great man is a Christian in belief —. 〈かつてギリシャ人やエジプト人は両者とも高度に文明化された人々でキリスト教とは異なった神々を信じていた。後にローマ人やギリシャ人は高度に進んだ文明をもってはいたが外国の信仰を受容していた。しかしその後この高度文明人は異なった信仰をもった民族に征服された。マホメット教はかつて最も高い文明を誇っていた宗教であった。またある時にはインドの宗教は最も高度に文明化された宗教であった。ある民族の文明がそれが何であれ宗教と何らかの関係があるかどうかは疑わしい。— さらに、キリスト教国ではもっとも教養ある人々はキリスト教は信じてはいない。そしてキリスト教も無数の宗派に分かれてお互いに憎みあっている。ヨーロッパのすぐれた科学者も — 高名な哲学者も — そして真に偉大な人物は信仰において誰一人としてクリスチャンではない。〉

* ここでハーンは古代のギリシャやエジプト文明下では多くの神々への信仰が一般であったことを指摘する。ローマは4世紀にキリスト教を国教にして政教一致で国家の基礎を固めた。しかしこの帝国はゲルマン民族によって分裂させられた。チュートン族の神話をもつゲルマン民族は低地ドイツの地域から来た素朴な多神教徒であった。そして歴史上キリスト教は多くの派（セクト）に分かれて時に激しい宗教戦争を引き起こした。ここからハーンは文明と宗教の必然的なつながりについて疑問を呈する。しかし「すぐれた科学者」「著名な哲学者」「真に偉大な人物」は誰一人としてキリスト教徒ではなかった、とコメントしている点はいささか極端かもしれない。ここにはハーンのキリスト教に対する公平さを欠く視点があるといえる。問題はむしろハーンの中にあってここまでキリスト教嫌いにさせたものにこそ思いを馳せなければならないと思われる。

〈8〉 科学

Biology is the Science of Life — how plants and animals grow and propagate, and why they have special shapes, colors, or habits — and the chemistry of digestion, blood making, etc. 〈生物学は生命の科学である。—それは植物や動物がどのように育ち、繁殖するか、また、なぜ彼らは特異な形、色、習性を持っているかを調べるもの—しかも消化、造血等の化学なのである。〉

* ハーンはニューオーリンズ滞在中にハーバート・スパンサーの思想に出会っている。この考えはダーウィンの生物学的進化論を社会発展の説明原理として応用しようとするものであった。かくしてハーンは自然淘汰の原理を認め、国や個人も生き残るためには知

恵や力による適応力を必要とすることを認めていた。「生物学」を説明するのに「生命の科学」すなわち進化論的な背景において生き物たちの特異な色や形や習性にはそれなりの理由があることをハーンは生徒にコメントするのであった。ここで生物学にはハーン自身深い関心を寄せていたことが窺える。

まとめ

　ラフカディオ・ハーンが明治23年（1890）に来日後松江で英語教師として教壇に立ち、生徒たちの英作文に添削を加え、返却したものが時を経てガラス乾板という形で今日見ることができることはひとつの驚きであり、喜びである。生徒たちの書いた英語そのものへの加筆・修正のコメントは言うまでもなく多くあるが、それ以外に生徒が書いた文章の内容に触れて余白の箇所にさまざまな評（コメント）や助言（アドバイス）を惜しまず与えていることは注目に値する。
　本書は熊本県立図書館で見つかったハーンの松江時代の英語（英作文）の授業で二人の生徒（大谷正信、田辺勝太郎）の書いたものに彼自身がコメントあるいはアドバイスしたガラス乾板の内容を判読・復元・日本訳を行い、これをさらに分類・分析してみたものである。第一にハーン先生がどのような先生であったのかについて木下順二の若き日（五高生時代）に書いた論考を参照にしながら述べた。第二に課題（テーマ）としてハーンが生徒に課したものを大谷正信、田辺勝太郎それぞれの生徒の分を紹介し、これを包括的に分類してみた。第三に実際のハーンによって余白に書かれたコメントやアドバイスの具体例を示しながらそれぞれについて筆者のコメントを付け加えた。ここではハーンが特にスペースを割いているテーマのうち際立ったものを記載した。本書で紹介・分析した内容は「語源」「敵者生存の原理」「キリスト教」「神道と仏教」「信仰と礼儀」「創造者」「文明と宗教」「科学」の8ジャンルであった。
　ハーンは来日後教育現場に立って生徒の書いた英作文から取材的な態度によって日本のことをよく学び理解を深めた。同時に彼は生徒一人一人に対して懇切丁寧な英語の文法的・語法的修正に加えて内容に関しても懇切丁寧なコメントを行っていた。本書の目的はハーンが行った英作文の授業で二人の生徒に施した訂正やコメントのガラス乾板の判読・復元・日本語訳を通してその実際の姿を少しでも明らかにすることであった。課題として出されたテーマを分類してみると如何にも日本的なものが出ており、生徒は経験的に書きやすく、ハーンは卑近な日本の文化や伝統に触れて大いに有益であったろうし、書かれたハーンのコメントの内容を分析してみるとハーンは教壇にあって一貫して学生に対しては同じ目線に立ち、共感と励ましのスタンスをもって臨んでいたことがよく分かるのである。

（西川盛雄）

＊　なお本章は『ラフカディオ・ハーン《近代化と異文化理解の諸相》』（九州大学出版会、2005年）に掲載されたものに加筆修正を加えたものである。

〈参考文献〉

洗川暢郎（1991）「ラフカディオ・ハーンと理科教育観」『へるん』28号、pp. 17-19.
太田雄三（1994）「ラフカディオ・ハーン―虚像と実像―」岩波新書

角田洋三（1996）「教師としてのハーン」『へるん』33号　pp.7-9．
木下順二（1935）「小泉八雲先生と五高」『五高同窓会々報』第8号
小泉　凡（1995）「民俗学者・小泉八雲」恒文社
梶谷泰之（1990）「ハーンを怒らせた学生」『へるん』27号　pp.34-36.
篠田一士、千石英世、寺島悦恩（訳）（1987）「西洋落穂集」『ラフカディオ・ハーン著作集第四巻』恒文社
千石英世（1987）「ジャーナリストとしてのハーン」『ラフカディオ・ハーン著作集第四巻』恒文社
高木大幹（1978）「小泉八雲と日本の心」古川書房
高橋節雄（1965）「松江時代のハーン先生の授業ぶり」『へるん』第1号
田部隆次（1980）『小泉八雲』（第4版）北星堂書店
西野影四郎（2000）「教師ヘルン（二）」『へるん』37号　pp.36-38
根岸磐井（1933）『出雲における小泉八雲』松江八雲会発行（再改訂増補版）
野口米次郎（1926）『小泉八雲傳』第一書房
萩原順子（1991）「ラフカディオ・ハーンと語学教育」『へるん』28号　pp.14-16
平川祐弘（1988）『小泉八雲とカミガミの世界』文藝春秋社
平川祐弘（2004）『ラフカディオ・ハーン』ミネルヴァ書房
丸山　學（1936）『小泉八雲新考』北星堂書店

後　記

　ラフカディオ・ハーン(小泉八雲)は来日後しばらく横浜に滞在したが、やがて明治23年(1890) 9月から明治24年(1891) 10月にかけて島根県尋常中学校にあって、英語教員として教壇に立つ教育者であった。その間日本について調べ、理解し、これを文章化して西洋に送るという仕事を終始怠らなかった。熊本で発刊された *Glimpses of Unfamiliar Japan*(『知られぬ日本の面影』)はハーン来日後の具体的な成果である。その背景には、ハーンは来日前のシンシナティやニューオーリンズのアメリカ時代やフランス領西インド諸島のマルティニーク時代には有能なジャーナリストとして活躍していたことが大きく影響を与えていると考えられる。

　教壇ではハーンは生徒と同じ目線に立ち、生徒たちに対して共感の心をもち、彼らによく慕われていた。そのハーンは英語の英作文の時間に彼らにとって身近な課題(テーマ)で自由英作文を書かせ、それを丁寧に添削して生徒に返却していた。生徒からすると英語力向上の契機となり、ハーンからすると日本文化の現状や自然や若者気質についての＜取材＞の一環として日本を理解するためのよい契機となるものであった。

　平成16年(2004) 6月にハーンの松江時代の教え子、大谷正信と田辺勝太郎の二人の生徒の英語添削文のガラス乾板が熊本県立図書館で見つかった。ガラス乾板の英文は学生の書いた英作文とハーンがこれに添削・コメントを書き加えたものである。すべてハンド・ライティングであり、第三者がこれを読む事を想定しておらず、教育者としてのハーンの特徴が直接顕著に出ているものである。ガラス乾板の文字は判読し難い部分も多かったが、その資料的価値の大きさに鑑みてこれを判読・復元し、その日本語訳を行うことはハーン研究上必須のことであった。作成した下書き原稿はネイティヴ・スピーカーの視点も加えて何度も見直し、検討して判読と復元の正確を期した。

　松江時代・熊本時代の教育者ハーンについて語られることは多い。しかし説得力をもって具体的な一連の生の資料に基づく説明はそう多くない。本書は生徒が書いた英作文にハーン自身が手を入れ、まずは英文を訂正し、さらに生徒に対しては有益なコメントを随所に書き込んだものである。これを掘り起こし、分類・分析することによってハーンの英語教師としての姿勢や生徒たちへの思いが具体的に分かるのである。本書に入れた論文はこの主旨に沿ったものである。

　本書は旧来の教育者ハーン研究についての先行研究を参考にしながらも新たに発見された具体的資料の紹介という意味合いを持つ。この書がハーンの顕彰と研究において新たな一石を投げかけることになれば幸いである。

　本書が出来上るまでにさまざまな方のお世話になった。本書に貴重な序文をお寄せ下さったハーン曾孫の小泉凡先生にはまず心より御礼申し上げたい。また本書で用いたハーン先生による英語の添削文のガラス乾板は熊本県立図書館(近代文学館併設)が所蔵・保管しており、同館の理解とご協力なくしてはこの作業は成しえなかった。また本書は「熊本大学学術出版助成」制度の支援を得て成ったものであり、ここに同大学に深く感謝の意を表するものである。さらにテキストの判読・復元作業のなかで熊本大学・学術資料調査研究推進室々員、文学部・福澤清教授と文学部・教育学部の大学院学生諸君のお世話になった。記して謝意を申し述べたい。また本書は2010年3月に報告書として出したものを大幅に修正・改訂を加え、このたびの製本に至ったものであ

る。なお出版をお引き受けいただいた弦書房の小野静男氏、野村亮氏には細かいところまでいろいろお世話になった。心より感謝申し上げる次第である。

平成23年(2011) 3 月31日
アラン・ローゼン
西川盛雄

〈編著者略歴〉

アラン・ローゼン（Alan. D. Rosen）

1945年生まれ。1967年ペンシルベニア大学英文科卒業、1972年ブリン・モー大学大学院文学研究科博士（PhD）課程修了。元熊本大学教授。
主要論文・著書：『ロックの心1、2、3』（共著、大修館、1982～85）, "Hearn and the Gastronomic Grotesque" (*Rediscovering Lafcadio Hearn*, Global Books, 1997)、『小泉八雲作品抄』（共著、恒文社、1999）、「ラフカディオ・ハーンの科学論説I、II」（『ハーン曼荼羅』、北星堂、2008）, "In the Drawer of his Mind": The Works Hearn Never Wrote" （八雲会、2010、『へるん』46号）。

西川盛雄（にしかわ・もりお）

1943年生まれ。1969年大阪大学大学院文学研究科修了、1973年ミネソタ大学大学院留学、1985年英国ランカスター大学大学院留学。専攻は英語学／言語学・異文化理解。現在熊本大学客員教授／名誉教授。
主要論文・著書：『ラフカディオ・ハーン＝近代化と異文化理解の諸相＝』（編著、九州大学出版会、2005）、「異界の創造＝ラフカディオ・ハーン＝」（『〈異界〉を創造する』（阪大英文学会叢書3）、英宝社、2006）、『英語接辞研究』（開拓社、2006）、『ハーン曼荼羅』（編著、北星堂、2008）、「『ゴンボ・ゼーブ』の三層構造」（新曜社、2009、『講座小泉八雲II』）。

ラフカディオ・ハーンの英作文教育
Lafcadio Hearn's Student Composition Corrections

2011年4月25日第1刷発行
2013年8月30日第2刷発行

著　者　アラン・ローゼン
　　　　西川盛雄
発行者　小野静男
発行所　弦書房
　　　　〒810-0041　福岡市中央区大名2-2-43 ELKビル301
　　　　TEL 092-726-9885　FAX 092-726-9886
　　　　E-mail:books@genshobo.com
　　　　http://genshobo.com/
印　刷　アロー印刷株式会社
製　本　篠原製本株式会社

© 2011
落丁・乱丁本はお取替えいたします
ISBN978-4-86329-057-0 C0021